A
Bunny
for
Easter

 2025

A.E. JENSEN *and* **E.L. OUGH**

A Bunny for Easter

Cover Design: Jenn ReadsBooks

Cover images: Canva, Pexels

Beta reader: Regitse Liljadorff

Editing and Formatting: Jenn ReadsBooks

Formatting images: Canva, Creative Fabrica

Blurb

Bunny

April is the cruellest month...

Isn't that how the poem goes? At least it's always been true for me. An Easter baby, I've been an inconvenience to my parents from the day I was born. From nasty words to pure indifference, my childhood was something I didn't like to revisit. Especially not that dreadful day when they took my bunny away from me...

But luckily, that's all in the past! I have a new job—my dream job, actually—in a chocolate shop, and my new boss, Easter Bennett, is the dreamiest guy to have walked the face of the earth, *ever*. He's a little grumpy, though... well, a lot, actually, and I often find him looking at me funny when he thinks I don't notice.

Sometimes I wonder if he is 'The One.' The one I can finally let my guard down with and be myself. The one I can introduce to Bunny. Because being around my new boss has Bunny begging to come out. He's pleading to be set free so he can be owned by him, my Master.

*A **Bunny for Easter** is a sweet and spicy MM novella and the third book in the* Kinked for the Holidays *series. It features a lost, neglected Bunny who finally finds his Master in a dashing, yet awfully grumpy, chocolatier in small-town Kent. Expect fluffy bunny ears, onesies with easy access, multi-purpose carrots, and chocolate play when opposites collide, and two lonely souls find their happily ever after.*

Content Warnings & Reader Advisory

A Bunny for Easter is an MM romance novella with explicit sexual content and, therefore, intended for a mature audience only. Some of the warnings below may act as spoilers, but they are there for a reason. Mental health matters:

- Emotional/verbal abuse by a main character's parents

- Mentions of losing a pet as punishment from parents

- Mentions of the death of a parent during childhood

- Brief mentions of homelessness and hunger

- Explicit sexual content featuring an ongoing bunny/master dynamic, including costumes and role-play

- Mentions of childhood bed wetting including one on-page scene in present time (adulthood)

Authors' Note

Dear readers,

If you've picked up A *Bunny for Easter*, it means that either a) our gorgeously stunning promo worked or b) you really can't get enough of the Kinkster Sisters and our crazy ramblings. And yes, we're allowed to use the term *crazy* because we both have proof—on paper—that we are outside what is considered the norm.

Anyway, Bunny and Easter's story has been underway for a while because, you know, life. But now it's finished and we hope that you'll love it as much as we do. There aren't many Easter romance books out there, but the authors are of the opinion that Easter is a *very* sexy holiday because, you know, chocolate. There's so much fun stuff that you can do with Easter (said the naughty little Bunny, *snort*); bunny ears, bunny tails, bunny onesies, and... yeah, you get the point. All the pretty flowers start bursting from the barren ground and the pretty pastels are just everywhere. There are birds' songs and just hope in general. *Optimism*.

And we can all use a little optimism and hope for the way this world is right now. It's not always a good place for people like us. For people like Bunny and Easter. But we hang in there and we forge ahead. We <u>will</u> **not** be silenced. Because as long as hope and an invincible human spirit exist, there are things to look forward to and lives to be led, regardless of if you're queer or *'outside the norm.'*

It's not a coincidence that we went with the grumpy/sunshine theme. Because Easter needed a little sunshine in his life. It's also not a coincidence that we once again went with the good old hurt/comfort, because who hasn't been hurting and longed for comfort once or twice in their life? There's a little age gap, too, because that's apparently how we roll.

And there's a little pee. Not a lot, just a little. Because as you may know from our previous books and solo projects, a lot of our inspiration comes from our own lives. And that's also the case with the pee. We all do it, but for some of us, it's more serious than that. It's linked to our trauma. It's part of something we carry with us. Something that can be shameful and make us feel less. Unworthy perhaps. But it's not shameful. It's a physical reaction to something that's not okay. It's the child's way of saying, "See me, listen to me, I'm hurting, but I can't tell you, because you don't listen and you don't care."

At least, that was the way it was for me, Anja. I used to wet my bed as a child, almost every night, up until I was 11 or 12. It was my body's reaction to a chaotic home with substance and emotional abuse. It was beyond my control and still, I carried the shame with me all the way through my childhood. I never had sleepovers. It was impossible. I never told anyone. No-one outside my house knew about it. This is the first time I'm sharing it with anyone—because Bunny needed me to.

Anyway, this is not about us, this is about our beautiful Bunny and his Easter. It's about overcoming your trauma and finding love. And it's about the magic of chocolate and all things fluffy and pink and pretty. And we even put a little surprise in there for you! Because it's Easter and we love surprises! Enjoy!

Love,

Anja & Emma

Playlist

These are the songs we dreamt about, plotted out, and wrote when bringing
Bunny *and his* **East** *to life. You can find it on* **Spotify.**

My Crown *by Marius Bear*
My World *by Callum Scott*
Chocolate *by The 1975*
Better With You *by Veronica Fusaro*
It's Been a While *by Joya Marleen*
Carry Me Home *by Jorja Smith, Maverick Sabre*
Sweetest Thing *by Allman Brown*
Spring *by Angel Olsen*
Rush Rush *by Paula Abdul*
HAVE MY BABIES? *by Isaiah Falls*
Stay With Me *by Sam Smith*
Just Give Me a Reason *by P!nk, Nate Ruess*
Say You Won't Let Go *by James Arthur*
East *by Sleeping at Last*
Lavender *by Dreamer Boy*
Hold Back The River *by James Bay*
If You Ever Want To Be In Love *by James Bay*
Us *by James Bay*

Sunshine In The Room by James Bay, Jon Batiste
Spring Into Summer by Lizzy McAlpine
Lost Without You by Kygo, Dean Lewis
Just Love Me by Tiffany
Winter's Over by Tiffany
The Good Side by Troye Sivan
Angel by Finneas
LOVE LOOKS PRETTY ON YOU by Nessa Barrett
come out and play by Billie Eilish
listen before i go by Billie Eilish
Gorgeous by Kane Brown
You Took the Words Right out of My Heart by Dorothy Lamour
Love Me Harder by Ariana Grande, The Weeknd
Hold On, We're Going Home by Drake, Majid Jordan
Call Me Lover by Sam Fender
By My Side by Black Atlass, SONIA
Adventure of a Lifetime by Coldplay
ocean eyes by Billie Eilish
Lust for Life by Lana Del Rey, The Weeknd
BLEED by The Kid LAROI
Ordinary by Alex Warren
Bad Dreams by Teddy Swims
Sanctuary by Welshly Arms
Safe by Nico Santos

Dedication

To anyone who has ever been made to feel less than by the people who were supposed to love them unconditionally. May you find your true forever family and experience the happiness and love you deserve.

*Children are a gift, **never** an inconvenience.*

Chapter One

"Uhm...I'm here about the...the position. For the holiday help?"

For fuck's sake. What was supposed to be an easy task—hiring some extra help in preparation for Easter—has turned out to be a full-time shit show. Just my luck. I guess I just have to buckle up and work extra-long hours the weeks before the holidays. Yeah, well, it isn't exactly like I have places to be or people to see, anyway. Might as well just work myself into an early grave like my mum predicted.

'You'll work yourself into an early grave, Easter. When are you going to find a nice young girl and settle down?'

Cut to ten years later and I'm still single; no nice young girl—or boy, actually—in sight. My small business in rural Kent, which I started from scratch ten years ago, has become my only accomplishment in life, to my mum's eternal regret since she always envisioned a wife and kids for me. Even now, when I've reached the ripe old age of thirty-four, she won't let it go.

"Sorry. The position's been filled," I groan, brushing at the permanent *fuck my life* frown between my eyebrows. I swear, I wasn't born this way—this *people-loathing*, I guess you could call it. I think I used to be a happy kid and a somewhat agreeable teenager. I mean, I used to have friends, right? Boyfriends even. *'You're such a self-entitled prick, East. You're just so...argh! Fuck it! Fuck you, East! It's like talking to a wall. There's just...nothing!'* Yeah, well, maybe not. Maybe if I were to go by my latest in an endless row of failed relationships, I really just am an arse, plain and simple. At least, there wasn't the slightest trace of doubt in my ex-boyfriend Jude's eyes just before he slammed the door behind him. *Prick.* Yep, might as well just call a spade a spade, right?

"Oh...o-kay," a frail voice drifts through my small chocolate shop, *East of Eden*. Yeah, I know, pretentious much? But you might as well go big or go home, right? The young man in front of me shifts on his feet, his gaze drifting to the shelves behind me as he squeezes a crumpled piece of paper between his fingers compulsively. Bollocks, he looks like he's going to tip over at any second. Great, just what I need! Some... *kid* fainting in my shop when I'm already so far behind on my orders. The phone's been ringing on-off for most of the morning, one retail store after another asking when they can expect their delivery. Let me just check for you, madam... Ah yes, in the month of never in the year 2000 and a fat chance.

"What's *wrong* with you?" I snap, my voice reaching a new level of pissed off with a generous dash of unfriendliness that's harsh even for me.

"Uhm...do you...?" he mumbles, his flickering gaze coasting along the half-finished Easter display in the front window, a string of pastel-coloured Easter eggs looking sad and lonely against the grey sky. A few rays of frail sunlight reveal how the nasty spring weather has left its mark on the glass, reminding me I really ought to call my window guy, Steve. Only, after that awkward hand job in the storage room last time he was here, I'm not so sure it's a good idea. I don't think I can face Steve the Squealer again anytime soon.

"What do you mean?" the kid near-whispers, the puzzled softness of his voice tugging at something inside of me that has lain dormant for a decade or two.

"You look like you're about to have a seizure or something," I sigh, that blasting headache starting to show its face again.

"Oh, no sir, I'm just..." he pauses, turning his head in my direction, a pair of pale greyish-brown eyes connecting with mine. His curious stare tracks my hand as I rub it against that pounding spot in my forehead, right between my brows. Small beads of perspiration dot his forehead like tiny crystals, strands of damp chocolate-brown hair stick to his temples, and his cheeks painted a crimson red. He looks like he's run a fucking marathon in the desert at high noon. "Do you think I could have a glass of water before I leave, please?" He swallows audibly before licking his dry lips. "It's warmer outside than I thought and..." he drifts off, scrunching his nose, his eyes lingering on something on the wooden counter. "Is that..." he sucks in a clipped breath, an expression of awe on his face, light flashing through his unique eyes, his eyelashes fluttering in... *ecstasy?* "Are those *porcelana?*" He points a slim, pale finger at the bowl of cocoa beans displayed on the counter, his voice vibrating with a misplaced excitement that, for some reason, goes straight to my balls.

"Yes. How do you...?" I look at him, stupefied that this... *kid...* would know a cocoa bean from a kidney bean, let alone recognise one of the best cocoa beans in the world. I get them directly from the farmer, Juan, in a small village in Northern Venezuela—a place I've visited numerous times over the years. I don't want to rely on any middlemen. If you want the best quality, you have to go directly to the source. Twelve years in this business, first as the youngest chief chocolatier *ever* at the Lanesborough in London, and then on my own, have taught me that, amongst other things. Besides, this way Juan gets all the profit. "How do you know they're *porcelana?*" I counter, failing to hide the hint of admiration in my voice. Could be he's just name dropping for all I know. The young man looks at me timidly, a trace of guardedness in his eyes.

"Uhm...it's the colouring and the...the structure, sir." He wets his bottom lip, the tip of his pink tongue sweeping along its plumpness as he takes a careful step towards the counter. As he steps into the sparse light from the window, his flowy hair becomes alive, the richest, most chocolatey brown I've ever seen, with flecks of auburn in it, shimmering in the sunlight. For some reason, I gulp, my stomach doing a weird twirl. Nodding at the bowl, he murmurs, "Sir, may I?" I nod slowly, curious where this is going. For all I know, he could've read on my website that most of my chocolate is made from the exclusive *porcelana* bean.

Reaching the counter, he leans in over the bowl and inhales deeply, closing his eyes in the process, his eyelashes fluttering like the wings of tiny brown wrens. His nostrils flare briefly, a near inaudible sigh leaving his lips. "Sandalwood," he whispers, and I instinctively lean in closer to catch his words. "Just a hint of tobacco," he mutters to himself, scrunching his button nose, a few scattered freckles dancing across the ridge. "And..." he hesitates, the air positively sizzling with anticipation, "patchouli."

Patchouli. Never in a million years have I considered the word patchouli, its elusive meaning escaping me every time I've tried to describe the scent of this treasured bean. Sandalwood, yes. Tobacco, of course. But patchouli? Never has my mind gone in that direction, but there it is. As clear as fucking day, spoken by a... a *kid*, like it's the best-known truth in the world, when to me, it's a goddamn epiphany. *Pat-fucking-chouli.* Hallelujah.

"Patchouli," I repeat lamely, completely blindsided at ten-ish on a Tuesday morning on my own turf.

"Patchouli," he breathes, opening his eyes and brushing his index finger along the edge of the cream-coloured bowl. "Porcelain for *porcelana*," he blinks at me and the seductive way that his tongue wraps around the letter P sends fire racing down my thighs, licking at my skin. Holy fucking fudge filling. "It...*fits*," he concludes, leaning up again. It *fits*. The words echo through my chest, accompanied by the frantic *thump, thump, thump* of my heart. "Thank you for your time, sir," he interrupts my thoughts, looking at me as if I somehow hold the answer to every question he's ever had. And I have... *nothing.* Absolutely nothing. My mind has gone entirely blank. *It. Fits.* "I've already taken up more than enough of your valuable time."

As he turns towards the door, his slim shoulder briefly brushes against my chest, and I'm awoken from my stupor like someone's just poked me with a stun gun. Like an idiot, I blink my eyes a couple of times before nodding at the paper that he's still clutching furiously in his right hand, his knuckles white.

"Let me see that," I blurt gruffly, nodding at the paper. He freezes on the spot, looking down at his hand as if it isn't even a part of him, his eyes mirroring confusion.

"But...I thought..." he gasps, his eyelids blinking rapidly.

"Call it a momentary lapse of...*something*," I murmur, my voice softening just a tad as I brush my fingers along the wrinkled paper, taking it from his hand. Turning towards the counter, I gesture at him to follow me, and he trails after me reluctantly. Smoothing the paper out against the plain surface of the dark cherrywood counter, I take in the handwritten lines in front of me. It's been a while since I've seen a handwritten CV, a simple pencil, such a foreign concept to this generation of TikTokkers and digital delinquents. There's something delicate—endearing even—about the slope of the individual letters, an almost juvenile dedication in every syllable. In places, the pencil has almost pinched a hole in the paper as if he has used excessive force—or passion perhaps—writing the CV. Fuck. Me.

Benjamin B. Sable it says at the top of the paper, the B slightly tilted as if his hand slipped writing it. My cock throbs and I just manage to suppress a whine of what I'm sure would have been pitiful at best.

"Sable?" I repeat aloud, feeling his soft breath against my chin. In my newfound appreciation of good penmanship, I hadn't realised that he's come to a stop unbelievably close to me, leaning in over my shoulder, observant of my every move and action.

"Yes," he nods eagerly, a rebellious brown curl bouncing against his forehead. This close, I notice his coat is worn to the point of threadbare and someone has attempted to repair it in places with rough, irregular stitches. It feels wrong somehow, perhaps even a mockery, that someone this pretty—because Benjamin B. Sable is *very* pretty, no doubt about it—should wear something this old and worn. "Like the rabbit, sir," he continues, completely oblivious as to what he's doing to me with that recurring *sir*.

"The rabbit?" *Sweet baby Jesus in a chocolate fountain.* "Yes, the rabbit breed. *Sable.*" Fuck, the way he pronounces the word. So breathy and... sultry, almost. There's a strange seductiveness about his voice that entirely contradicts the plain innocence of his appearance. His beige cable-knit sweater peeks from behind his coat and equally worn grey woollen pants. His sensible brown leather boots. His light lavender scarf, wrapped neatly around his slender neck, is the only thing adding a hint of colour to his attire. As his lips curl into a pout at the end, a strained rumble grows in my throat, and I quickly disguise it with a small cough.

"Of course," I sigh, shaking my head. I continue reading, painfully aware of the proximity of this Benjamin B. Sable person. "What does the B stand for?" I feign indifference when, really, I'm dying to know. Like my future happiness depends solely on that B and what it means.

"I...I don't know," he squeaks, shifting next to me.

"What do you mean, you don't know?" I ask, my patience wearing thin, that tempting breath of his coasting across my chin, making my body recall all sorts of long-forgotten sensations. Standing this close, I'm painfully aware of the delicate slope of his chin and the pink hue to the tip of his right earlobe, the pink starting to bleed further down his neck. *I did that. I made him blush.* A ridiculous, immature sense of pride courses through me, and I quickly collect myself.

"No one ever told me, sir," he states matter-of-factly. "And I never asked." He shrugs, his gaze downcast as if he's almost waiting for me to disapprove of him or tease him about it. An unfamiliar feeling of unrest rises inside me. For some reason, I suddenly feel angry, and I don't know why or at whom. I'm just angry. *No one ever told me.* Shit. I continue reading, trying to focus on the words in front of me.

Date of Birth: April 15th, 2001.

"You're an Easter baby," I blurt, my mouth going all rogue on me. *Easter baby? For the love of God, pull yourself together, East.*

"Yes," he nods. "Easter Sunday, sir," he adds, his voice quivering. "It was quite...inconvenient..." he trails off, avoiding my stare.

"Inconvenient?" I repeat brusquely. I really am an old arsehole.

"Yes," he nods solemnly. "I shouldn't have come around until after the holidays," he says. "So, as you see, quite inconvenient, sir." He articulates every syllable carefully, almost as if they carry some sort of special meaning to him. Perhaps they do. I just feel increasingly angrier, my fingers threatening to tear his CV apart. *Inconvenient. How can a child be fucking inconvenient? That's a load of bollocks.* Unexpected houseguests are inconvenient. A fucking blizzard or a delayed train, yes. But a child? Although I don't have nor do I particularly want some of my own, I am, however, of the firm belief that you should only acquire a child if you truly desire one. Taking a deep breath to stave off the anger that's slowly but steadily turning into wrath of biblical proportions, I read on, the letters dancing in front of me.

Skills and Qualifications:

1. Easter specialist

2. Vast knowledge of cocoa beans

3. Online Master Class completed in tempering chocolate

4. Extensive knowledge of fillings and decorating techniques...

Jesus fucking Christ, why am I even contemplating this? This... *inconvenient kid*, this Benjamin-I-don't-know-what-the-B-stands-for has disaster-waiting-to-happen written all over him. He may as well have a big fat NO! stamped on his forehead. And yet, I find myself carefully folding the paper together, placing it in the front pocket of my charcoal linen apron, and speaking the words I would least expect, "So, Benjamin B. Sable, when can you start?"

Chapter Two

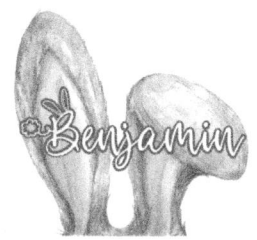

W hat does one wear for the first day of work as a shop assistant in one of the most well-renowned chocolatiers in the UK? And why didn't I just ask my new boss Mr Bennett what the appropriate attire for such an esteemed position would be? *You know why, Benjamin. Because you were too busy smelling him, ogling him, dreaming of...* Yes, yes, I know, but oh gosh, was he dreamy looking. I mean, a little standoffish and grumpy, but oh so very, *very* handsome. Dashing, actually. With his golden-blond hair and clear blue eyes. I wonder how old he is. He seemed old because he was very serious, but I didn't notice any grey in his hair, although it was rather hard to tell because it was oh so very golden. And his skin... beautiful and soft-looking, with a few fine lines around his eyes.

Trailing my fingers along the different coloured dress shirts displayed on a table in the high street shop, *Meredith's Modern Men's Wear*, I recall what Mr Bennett was wearing. Dark jeans. A navy-blue button-up. And that charcoal apron wrapped around his broad chest and slim midsection, the grey colour clashing with the icy blue of his inquisitive eyes. His gaze wasn't hostile per se, just intense. It felt like he could see right through me, into the very core of me, peeling off the top layer of my well-rehearsed polite persona, only to reveal all my flaws and failures. All my mishaps and mistakes. Because there are indeed many, and my shortcomings were always thrown at me at every opportunity during my childhood.

'Look at you, Benjamin. Always such a mess. Can't go an entire day without messing up to save your life, can you?' and then, of course, Father's preferred phrase: 'You even had to ruin your mother's Easter luncheon, didn't you? It'd have been easier for everyone if you'd never been born.'

It's true, though. It would've been easier. At least, there's never been any doubt in my heart that my parents felt that way because they never failed to point it out every chance they got. And over the years, my brothers learned how to copy my parents' behaviour to get in their good graces. Needless to say, I haven't had any contact with any of them since the day I left home at eighteen.

"Can I help you, love?" A cheery voice sounds next to me, a pair of friendly grey eyes regarding me.

"I'm just...I'm just looking, thank you," I murmur, letting go of the soft cotton fabric. Lavender with a frail bluish undertone. My favourite colour.

"Well, if there's anything, then do let me know. I'm Meredith and this is my shop," she beams. *Oh, blast.* It's never easy—well, almost impossible, really—to steal from someone once you know their name. And *Meredith* is such a lovely name, and she even seems lovely. It's even harder if they treat you with kindness. I'm addicted to kindness, you see. Growing up without any can turn even the strongest of us into a kindness junkie. I don't

shoplift very often, but sometimes, when I see something very pretty and fluffy usually, the urge strikes.
"I uhm...Can I ask you something?" I lower my voice,
throwing a glance at the only other customer in the
shop. I've never been to this place before, although
it's on the high street in Nettle Green in Kent where
I've lived all my life. Maybe it's new.

"Of course you can, love," Meredith chirps.

"What would you wear for your first day of work as
a shop assistant in a chocolate shop? A high-quality
chocolate shop," I hastily add, shifting nervously on
my feet. The worn leather of my old shoes is soft
against my feet, but as much as I love them, they're
doing a poor job of hiding that they're falling apart.

"Well..." Meredith's smile is friendly as her eyes
coast along the row of dress shirts. "I would go
for smart but practical. It needs to give off a good
first impression since you're dealing with customers,
but it also needs to be something that you can
move around in freely." She taps her bottom lip
deep in thought before she reaches for a dark green
long-sleeved polo on a shelf next to her. "This one,
dear. Try this one. The moss-green will go perfectly
with your hair colour and your beautiful eyes," she
practically glows while handing me the polo.

Beautiful. No one has ever used the word beautiful
while referring to my eyes—or any other part of me,
for that matter.

*'Stop looking at me like that, with those beady eyes of
yours. You only have yourself to blame.'* Yes, it's true.
It is my fault. All of it. Looking down at the green
polo, I reach for it and the tips of my fingers connect
with the silky-soft fabric. So similar to Bunny's fur. So
smooth and warm and just overall lovely. *No. Don't go
there, Benjamin. Don't.*

"It's...it's very delicate," I whisper, a lump building in the back of my throat, the ghost of Bunny's sweet familiar scent lingering in my nostrils. "But it's too nice..." I trail off. "I'll only ruin it."

"Nonsense!" Meredith quips, her pearl earrings dangling cheerily. "A stunning young man like yourself. You need something nice to wear."

"I...I think I'll just wear something of my own. But thank you!" I rush out. The last thing I want is to hurt Meredith's feelings since she's been so nice to me. Nicer than anyone in a long time, really. Stealing a glance at the price tag only confirms that there's no way I can afford to buy the polo and now that I know Meredith, there's no way I can bring myself to lift it.

"Try it on, at least," she smiles, squeezing my left wrist. "See how it looks on you." Her expression is forthcoming, unjudging, with nothing but sincerity in her eyes. Suddenly, I want to see myself in it. Feel the fabric against my skin. To lose myself in another version of my life for just a moment, pretending that I'm someone else. That I *can* be someone else for, however briefly, a moment. Someone who wears delicately knitted moss-green polos and works in a prestigious chocolate shop alongside the—although slightly grumpy—very dashing Mr Bennett and doesn't have a single care in the world. Someone who's *not* Benjamin.

"Okay," I give in.

"Excellent," Meredith clasps her hands together in front of her chest, her fingernails painted in a pale pink mother-of-pearls varnish. "You're definitely a size small," she muses, leafing through the stack of polos. "Aha! Here we go. Last one. See, Lady Providence is smiling at us. The changing rooms are over there," she nods to the back of the shop. "If you need any help, love, just give me a shout and I'll be with you in a jiffy."

She turns around and walks towards the counter, her heels *click-click-clicking* against the grey epoxy floor, and I head in the other direction, towards the changing rooms.

Closing the curtain behind me, I quickly discard my worn mustard-coloured sweater on the wooden stool in the corner and carefully slide on the polo. Taking in my reflection in the full-size mirror, I freeze on the spot. The polo fits me perfectly, like a second skin almost. And Meredith was right. The deep moss-green colour really matches my dark brown hair perfectly. Even the dull brown of my eyes no longer seems quite so lifeless, but instead rather... pretty. Yes, pretty. The luxurious fabric stretches across my slim chest and tapers down my slender waist, and I suddenly like what I see in the mirror. I look stylish. Nice, even. And that's exactly it, isn't it? It's *too* nice. Too nice for someone like me.

'*Look what you've done, Benjamin. Ugh, you just ruin everything, don't you? No wonder your mother has stopped inviting people over when you're around. Such a nuisance.*' My heartbeat fastens into a frantic pace as the sound of Father's voice rings through my head. Yeah, I can't have nice things. I'll only ruin them just like I've ruined everything else.

Taking off the polo carefully, I quickly put my sweater back on and leave the changing area. Heading for the counter, my eyes downcast, I hope Meredith won't be there, so I can just place it on the counter and slip out of the shop unnoticed. No such luck, though.

"How was it?" she enquires cheerfully, twisting her golden necklace around her index finger.

"It was...it was very nice," I gulp, looking at the stack of woollen scarfs in pastel colours adorning the counter, my gaze zeroing in on a lemon meringue one. My mouth waters. I love pastels. I dream of an entire closet filled with pastel-coloured clothes. Like that scene in the *Great Gatsby*. The original one, not that awful, fast-paced one with Leonardo. No, the one with dreamy Robert Redford and Mia Farrow. When he shows her all her pastel-coloured shirts, she twirls around and laughs and laughs and lau—

"And...?" Meredith beams expectantly.

"Oh. I think I'll just think about it," I whisper, placing the polo on the counter and, along with it, my dream of life's little luxuries. "But thank you for your time."

"Nonsense! What's to think about? It's perfect for you, young man." A frown appears between her groomed brows as something seems to dawn on her. Brushing at her fringe, she bites her bottom lip, deep in thought, before her face suddenly brightens again. "Oh, silly me! I forgot to tell you. It's on sale. 50% off. I'm trying to make room for the new spring collection, so it's gotta go, really," she smiles as she starts to fold the polo neatly. "You sure I can't tempt you? Last small one in green," she sing-songs.

"I..." I lift my gaze, my eyes connecting with hers briefly. "I think I'll just..." I pull at the neckline of my sweater, a suffocating feeling rising in my chest, as I steal a glance towards the exit.

"I tell you what," she continues, unfazed, as she pulls a paper bag from behind the counter and places the polo inside it. "Take the polo. Then, when you get your first salary, you come pay me." There's a finality to her words, a challenging glimmer in her eyes, giving off an *end-of-discussion* message.

"But...but you don't know me," I blurt, my eyes stinging with unshed tears. "I'm just..." I shake my head in disbelief as she pushes the bag across the counter against my chest.

"And I *love* chocolate!" she coos. "It's my guilty pleasure, you see." She winks conspiratorially. For a moment, confusion blurs my mind. "And I don't mind a bit of liquor inside, if you know what I mean," she grins. "*Barnaby* is always better with a little buzz." She laughs, waving a hand in front of her. "Who am I kidding? Life in general—and menopause in particular—is better with a little buzz."

"Oh...I see..." I nod eagerly, leaning in over the counter and lowering my voice. "I don't think I'll get paid for another month, though."

"That's perfectly all right, love. You go on now." She shoos me, pointing at the exit. Still in somewhat of a stupor, I turn around and nearly float out of the shop, clutching the paper bag against my chest like it's my most prized possession. Well, it is. I've never owned anything this pretty before. If I had a closet, I would twirl and twirl and twirl around in front of it later, holding the polo against my chest. Just as I'm closing the door carefully behind me, she calls out after me, "And best of luck at your new job, young man! I hear our Mr Bennett is quite a character." *Yeah, I'm going to need that. I'm going to need all the luck in the world. But maybe—with this shirt—I can at least fool Mr Bennett for a little. Our Mr Bennett.*

Chapter Three

It's official then. My favourite colour is green. Moss green, to be exact. Damp, soft moss covering the forest bed after a light spring drizzle. Deep brown locks of hair resting against it, pale, near-translucent grey-brown eyes tipped towards the equally grey sky, creamy-white skin peeking from behind the collar of a moss-green shirt, pink lips shaped into an obscene O. And... *right.* If there's a colour in hell aside from flaming red like the flames currently licking up my inner thighs, I bet it's green, sent here to torture me in the middle of my own shop.

"You were—"

"What?!" I snap, my eyes dislodging from Benjamin's collarbone, evident behind that cursed green neckline. It's good quality. I can tell by the way the fabric drapes against his skin, the way it caresses his bones and cradles his... stop it, Easter! Will you just stop already? You know how this song goes.

"Sorry, Mr Bennett, sir," he murmurs, his gaze flickering fucking everywhere, long eyelashes fluttering. I wonder if they flutter like that—*exactly like that*—when his lips are shaped into that O, his entire body engulfed in the throes of passion, a sweet moan curling from his mouth. I bet they do. I bet that O tastes just as sweet and tangy as candy oranges covered by the darkest, bitterest of chocolate, the filthy combination exploding on your tongue, your mind going momentarily blank.

"...chocolate. You were about to tell me about chocolate," he breathes, his cheeks reddening. *Cho-co-late.*

He articulates the word in—at least to my deranged ears—the most obscene way possible. Much too obscene anyway for a bleak Wednesday morning. A morning that will, from this day forward, be known as the day that Easter M. Bennett officially and irrevocably lost his bloody mind. He says it in that airy, gaspy way, like one would say, '*suck me*' or '*finger me*' or '*fuck me.*'

"...me?"

"What?" I croak, my vocabulary apparently now limited to that one word that doesn't rhyme with *twat* but really should. Twat. Why, oh bloody why, is the universe doing this to me? All I wanted was a bloody shop assistant. Famous last words, I guess.

"I..." he looks uncertain around the shop, twisting his hands nervously. "I was just...where do you want me, Mr Bennett, sir?" His grey-brown eyes search my face questioningly. *On the counter. Face down. Ass up. That stupid green shirt stuffed into your mouth while I stuff you from behind.*

"There. Uhm, right there is fine, Mr Sable," I near-groan. He looks at me, puzzled, because he's standing just inside the shop door.

"Here?" He tilts his head, brown locks caressing the collar of the shirt that shall not be mentioned. "Right here?"

"Yes."

"You want to teach me about chocolate right here, Mr Bennett, sir?" Oh, for fuck's sake, what's with the Mr and the sir? Like one isn't more than enough. This isn't a bloody Dickens novel.

"Yes," I bite out.

"But—"

"Look, Mr Sable. If you're going to argue with me on your very first day of work, we might as well just terminate our relationship right now." Yes, Easter, for the love of anything holy or unholy, let this boy go this very minute. *Do it!* But then it starts, a small quivering movement at first, at the right corner of his mouth until small waves of tremors move along his full bottom lip. He just manages to suck a small whimper back into his mouth before it escapes.

"Please, Mr Bennett, sir." He looks at me, genuine despair in his pale eyes. "Please don't fire me, sir." He takes a step forward, and I automatically take one back, bumping my back against the counter, sending my favourite porcelain bowl—containing my precious *porcelana*—flying to the floor with a loud crash. Shit. I really fucking liked that bowl. "Oh no," he cries out, his gaze dipping to the floor, his eyes tracking the beans scattered everywhere. "Oh, no! I'm so, so sorry, Mr Bennett, sir," he stutters as he drops to the floor. *He drops to the goddamn floor.* My floor. Scrambling forward on his knees—*on his fucking knees*—he crawls along the hardwood floor, his slim fingers impossibly white against the dark-washed boards. Clawing his way forward, he looks up at me. "Please, Mr Bennett, sir. I'm so, so sorry." He picks up a fragment of the bowl, cradling it in the palm of his right hand. "I'll replace it. I promise. Just..." he hesitates as two fat tears make their way down his red-stained cheeks. "Just, please don't let me go." *Don't let me go.* Fuck.

Something shifts inside me at that strangled plea. *Don't let me go.* Something unfamiliar but not entirely unpleasant tugs at my heartstrings, like determined fingers pulling at the strings of a harp. A strange tune moves through my body, a long-forgotten melody, soft strokes from a distant room, beckoning at me. *Don't let me go.* Realisation strikes as Benjamin reaches for the first bean. Well, two things at once, actually. I know what that B stands for. With absolute unwavering certainty, I know what it stands for. And second, there's no way I'll ever be able to let him go. Not when I've finally found him. Because there's no doubt, is there? It's him.

"Stop!" I order, the words slamming into Benjamin like a massive wave. He stops, his hand hovering just above the cocoa bean. Holding his breath, he remains frozen on his knees in front of me.

"Sir?" he whispers, his traitorous tongue peeking out, the tip swiping along his bottom lip.

"That's not how you pick up a *porcelana*, is it?" I say with an edge to my voice that makes my own skin crawl. What the bloody hell? However, Benjamin shakes his head eagerly, brown curls tumbling onto his forehead.

"No, sir," he rushes out, eyes wide, pupils blown black.

"Go ahead then. No time like the present." I nod at the floor.

"Yes, sir," he sniffs, eyeing the closest bean. And then he moves. Clasping his hands behind his back, knuckles white, he bends towards the floor, the tip of his nose brushing against the hard dark wood. Something explodes inside me, maybe, possibly, my heart or my brain, as the flames reach my loins, my cock swelling in my pants. I'm going to go to hell for this. I am. But I just can't seem to help myself. Not when he's on his knees for me like that. I can't.

"Sir?" he whispers, his mouth hovering just above the cocoa bean.

"Do it," I rasp, barely hanging on to my last inch of restraint, my balls heavy, my cock throbbing. It feels like the floor is opening beneath me, the walls of this century-old building dissolving into thin air; everything I've ever known to be true is now slipping through my fingers. I hold on to the edge of the counter, my fingers digging into the surface, as my world tilts, up becoming down, and down becoming up.

Benjamin opens his mouth, his lips quivering, his clasped hands twisting behind his back. Then he closes the gap between his face and the floor and sucks the bean into his mouth. A guttural groan leaves my lips, my balls drawing up, as my left hand flies to my crotch, squeezing my cock. I just manage to stave off my orgasm. *Just.* Benjamin doesn't move as his mouth closes around the *porcelana*; the outline of his frail shoulder blades visible behind the thin fabric of his shirt like small bony wings. He's shivering and oh so *very* beautiful. I somehow always knew that he would be. Beautiful. But not like this. Not this broken and perfect at the same time. *Perfect for me,* my heart sings greedily.

On instinct, I push away from the counter. Bending at the hips, I hold my hand out in front of his mouth, palm up. Turning his face upwards, his eyes lock onto mine. He blinks once, a silent question lingering in the greyish-brown. I nod. His lips separate, saliva sticking to the bottom one. Then he sticks out his tongue, the precious bean resting on the soft pink cushion like an offering. I nod again and he bends his head and drops the bean into my palm. It's wet and warm against my skin. Closing my hand around it, I reach out my other hand, hesitating. *It's still not too late,* a distant rational voice whispers inside my head. *You can still ask him to go. It's not too late.*

But the thing is, I don't want him to. I don't want him to leave now that I've finally found him. Because there's no doubt. It's him. I think I already knew it yesterday, my soul recognising him the minute he walked in the door, my mind only just catching up now. It's him. It's my—

"Thank you," I say, closing the gap between my hand and his head, brushing my fingers through his soft, silky hair, petting him. Benjamin purrs, leaning into my hand, his head chasing my touch as I dig the tips of my fingers into his scalp. *Lovely.* He's so lovely. I wonder if he feels it, too. The sudden shift. I think somehow, he must, the air sparkling all around us, the world as we know it now blown to smithereens. "Thank you," I repeat, reluctantly removing my hand from his hair, a rogue lock tangled around my ring finger, the deep brown vibrant against my skin.

He smiles at me, his eyes shimmering, spilling over with joy at my praise. Oh, there's no doubt. It most certainly is him. And so I tell him.

"Go on." I nod at the floor, at the beans that are now only the second most precious to me. "Go on, *Bunny.*" Startled, he sucks in a breath, his eyes turning just a shade darker, his nostrils flaring. Pink watercolour spills from his cheeks down to his chin and further down his neck until it disappears behind the green. Then he collects himself, a shy smile coasting along his lips. Those two words, the best fucking words in the English vocabulary, spilling from his mouth, "Yes, Master."

Chapter Four

M y life is a dream. It's a dream. Skipping down the
pavement as the spring sun dips behind the tree
line, I can't stop grinning like a loon. *Bunny.* He called
me Bunny, forever and always claiming that anonymous
B for himself. I'm Bunny. And he's—my palm flies to my
mouth, stopping a loud giggle—*Master.* Oh gosh, when
he called me Bunny, I got instantly wet, like a faucet
bursting, all my pent-up want spilling over. It's tricky to
skip when your dick is leaking into your pants, but I can't
exactly do my bunny hops in public. I'm not a weirdo.
Well, maybe I am, but not in public... at least not for the
most part.

I don't know what comes over me when I walk into Mr
Bennett's shop, but it's like Bunny wants to break free
and come out and play and do other silly stuff. Not just
bouncing around, but also nuzzling Mr Bennett's neck
or lying down and resting on top of his feet, purring
like a good little pet. Oh, how I long to be a good little
pet. Someone's pet. *Master's pet.* It's getting harder and
harder to contain myself around Mr Bennett, that's for
sure. Yesterday, I almost wiggled my nose in front of

him, real bunny-style. Luckily, I managed to disguise it with a sneeze.

I turn down River Lane towards the communal allotment where Mr Harvey has his small plot of land and where I've been staying for three years now. You're not supposed to live there; it's just a small vegetable patch really, with a shed for utensils and gardening tools, but I've got nowhere else to go. Mr Harvey doesn't mind, though. He's really old, like before television old, and when I stumbled upon his small garden in a fit of hunger, I found it overgrown, weeds quickly taking over everything. The thing is, Mr Harvey didn't get mad. Back then, three years ago, when I stole a carrot from his garden. I think that's why I didn't run like I usually do when people get mad. I just froze in the middle of his overgrown vegetable patch, nibbling on the earthy, crunchy carrot.

"You all right there, lad?" Mr Harvey squinted at me in the twilight. "Are you lost?" I just nodded furiously, the carrot crunching between my teeth. I was so hungry, and the garden was so full. I could tell even behind all the shrubs and weeds.

"I like your garden," I squeaked, looking around. "It's a little overgrown, but I like it."

"It's a bloody mess is what it is," Mr Harvey laughed. "Can't seem to keep up with the weeds no more. Not since the Missus left." He shook his head, wiping at his eyes. At that moment, I recognised a kindred spirit inside the older man. He, too, looked as lost as I felt. That realisation made me bold, and Bunny isn't usually bold.

"I can help," I quipped, nibbling eagerly on the last bit of carrot.

As it turned out, that sentence became life-changing altogether. I've been helping Mr Harvey for three years now. His garden is no longer a mess, but the envy of all the other plot-holders. It's immaculate and they all wonder how Mr Harvey, at his age, manages to maintain it like that. Well, I do. Or rather, Bunny does. At night, when all the other plot-holders go home to their cosy flats and houses, to their warm tea and comfy beds, Bunny comes out and does the gardening. When everything is quiet and abandoned, he hops around and keeps everything neat and tidy while nibbling on a carrot or two. I love that special time at night when the world goes quiet, and it's just me, Bunny. I have a small lantern, but by now, I know the tiny garden as well as my own pocket, and I move around quickly and efficiently, removing small weeds and sorting out a broken marker or two.

In exchange, I get to stay in Mr Harvey's old shed and eat as many veggies as I want. Sometimes, when Mr Harvey has been to the garden during the day to catch some sun or glower in the praise and attention from the other plot holders, he leaves a little something for me in the shed. A box of biscuits or a chocolate bar. A bag of salt and vinegar crisps on occasion because he knows those are my favourites.

It's not much, my little shed, but it's as close to a home as I've ever had. I feel safe among the gardening equipment. Safer than I ever felt in my parents' house, that's for sure. I never knew what would come flying at me—verbally, I mean—from either my parents or my two older brothers, Clive and Theo. Gardening tools, on the other hand, don't fly... not unless you throw them.

In a corner, next to a worn wobbly table, Mr Harvey has put one of those foldout beds for me to sleep on. He brought it one day out of the blue, along with the most amazing-looking crocheted blanket done in shades of yellow, brown, and orange. Real 70s style. I used to toss and turn in my bed at home, wondering why I was so alone in the world, so unloved by everyone, but since I found Mr Harvey, I sleep like the dead.

Mr Harvey has become like a dad to me. I know he's not, but in my mind, I pretend he is. Or a grandad, at the very least. In the beginning, he would pretend he wasn't bringing stuff from the thrift store to the shed on my account, but now, whenever he's found something that he thinks I can use or would make me happy, he's full-on beaming with happiness. Like that small dresser for my clothes or that zinc water basin for me to wash up in. Or when he found a used copy of *The Wind in the Willows* because I told him how I always loved that book. He could hardly contain himself. He even let me give him a little hug.

Mr Harvey has changed too. He doesn't look old or sad anymore—at least not when he's around me. He jokes now, that deep belly laugh of his filling the small shed, wrapping around me like a warm blanket. He can even joke about the missus now and how he's a real poor sod, the younger fitness instructor that she left with, because if she doesn't kill him with her cooking, then her sour mood is sure to.

I can't cook at the shed, obviously, since there's no power, but sometimes Mr Harvey brings me leftovers. They're still warm when he gets here—he lives just two streets over so it doesn't take him that long to walk. It's mostly simple meals like bangers and instant mash or some beans on toast, but it's not about the food, really. It's the gesture. It's a sign that Mr Harvey cares. He *cares* about me. He shows me in so many ways. Ways I didn't even know existed.

It was a few weeks after I'd moved into the shed when he came by. '*I noticed you passing my street the other morning,*' he wiped at his forehead with his old hand-kerchief.

'*Yeah? Where do you live then?*' I, of course, knew already because I looked Mr Harvey up because I'm a curious cat. But I didn't want to appear like a stalker. Because I'm not. I was just curious.

'*Just over on Henley Lane.*' I nodded carefully as he continued. '*The old white house with me banged up Ford in the front. The blue one.*'

'*Oh yes, I know which one. I pass it on my way to work, Mr Harvey.*'

'*Oh, I see. Where do you work then?*' He tilted his head, his old, kind eyes blinking at me with genuine interest.

'*The large Tesco down by the fire station. I work in the back. Storage and inventory and things like that.*' It was then that I told him that my dream was to one day work in a real shop, preferably one where they made and sold their own chocolate. Since my great passion in life is chocolate. I was never allowed to have any growing up because sugar would make me hyper and '*you're enough of a nuisance as it is, Benjamin. We don't need you all high and buzzing with sugar.*' But oh, how I love it.

'*That's nice.*' Mr Harvey nodded, smiling absentmind-edly as he seemed to ponder something. '*It's good to have dreams.*' He hesitated while looking a little sad. I couldn't help but wonder if Mr Harvey still had dreams or if you stopped having them once you got older. '*How are you getting on, then?*' he continued, looking around the small shed, and my stomach instantly sank. I was trying to keep it neat and tidy, but perhaps Mr Harvey regretted taking me in.

'*Good, Mr Harvey,*' I swallowed.

'*It's not much, laddy.*' He rubbed at the back of his head. '*You know, since you pass me house in the morning, anyway, you're...*' His gaze dropped to the floor as he wiped biscuit crumbs from his protruding stomach be-hind his old cardigan. '*If you ever need to use the washing machine or the bath or...*' He shrugged as he continued to brush at invisible crumbs. At that moment, I again felt like giving the old man a hug. Not just because he looked like he needed it, but because I did, too. Just to know what it felt like. To be hugged. No one ever hugged me in my childhood home. That wasn't a thing, at least not when it came to me. But I imagined it would be nice. To hug someone. *'Since you walk by, anyway. You're welcome to come by a little earlier, maybe? For a cuppa and...you know...to have a bath or something.'*

My eyes stung as I teared up. I'd been showering at Tesco until now. We had some basic staff showers in the back, but they were never very clean, and I didn't like sharing my private space with other people. It was always a quick affair, just to stay clean and presentable. My laundry, the little I had, I took to a laundromat downtown.

'I only do me laundry once a week, every Sunday, so if you left some on Fridays then I could pop them in with me own...' he trailed off.

'You would let me do that?' I whispered. Mr Harvey nodded, a blush creeping up his weather-beaten cheeks. *'Thank you,'* I murmured. *'Thank you, Mr Harvey.'* And then I did hug him, after all. Just an awkward side hug at first until Mr Harvey pulled me into a tight embrace. And it was every bit as lovely and magical as I'd ever imagined it would be; Mr Harvey smelling of mothballs and Earl Grey and everything good and right in the world. I guess he needed it, too. The hug. Or someone like me. Just like I'd needed someone like him. A kind stranger.

So yes, that's my life now. It's simple, but it's safe. No unexpected fit of rage like when Mother found me in the rose bed in my bunny costume. I was only picking roses for her; it was, after all, her birthday. Instead, I ended up ruining that too—her birthday—and they all ended up going out to dinner without me instead. No patronising speeches from Father either about how I needed to toughen up like my brothers. That people in town were giving him the odd stare because I was such a disgrace to him. How sometimes he wondered if I was even his own flesh and blood, because how could I be when I was such a weakling? Such a pathetic excuse for a boy.

So yes, I'll take simple and safe any day of the week over comfortable and cold. I have Mr Harvey and now I have Master too. Well, I don't *have him* have him. Not yet, anyway. But one day I will. I'm sure of it. It's just a matter of time before he lets go and calls me Bunny again. One day I'll be his Bunny for real. I just know it. I can feel it deep inside when I steal a sniff of him or when his deep, demanding voice wraps around me. It's him. There's no doubt in my heart. Mr Bennett is my Master, and I am his Bunny.

Chapter Five

B enjamin has been with me for a week now, and nothing inappropriate has happened... that is, if you don't count the cocoa bean incident where he crawled on his knees across the floor for me, and I called him *Bunny*. That was perhaps slightly unprofessional of me, but I've written it off as a momentary spell of insanity.

If I'm being honest, he's the perfect shop assistant. He's polite and efficient and intuitively knows what a customer needs on any given day. He already knows his way around the shop and storage room like he's been here for ages, and most times I barely formulate a thought or a request, and he springs from behind the counter or a window display with his breathy, ever-present, 'Yes, *Mr Bennett, sir?*'

I haven't called him Bunny since Porcelana-Gate, and he hasn't called me Master, either. The sheer inappropriateness of my shop assistant referring to me as *Master* still doesn't keep me from wishing he would again. I find myself holding my breath every time he speaks, wishing that the M in *Mr* would spill over into a pleading, gasped *Master* instead. But unlike me, apparently, Benjamin B. Sable is as professional as can be. As a result, I've already jerked off twice today in the staff toilet and I fear round three isn't far behind. Each time I come, it's with a choked '*Bunny*' on my lips, cock in hand, dignity on the floor. Fuck.

He's back at the Easter decorations, propped up on a small stool as he leans in over the large window. His shirt, blue not green this time, rides up whenever he tries to reach for the hook drilled into the ceiling. It's where I hang the large seasonal ornament, the centre-piece of my window display. His creamy, milky-white skin peeks out from the waistline of his dark pants, like peppermint crème oozing from a piece of dark choco-late. My mouth waters and I quietly chastise myself. I've got work to do, although my to-do list is growing shorter every day now that Bun—*Benjamin* is here.

Christ, he's back to fondling the bunny's ears. I caught him doing it yesterday, too, as he unpacked and un-wrapped the Easter decorations, *oohing* and *aahing* over every little paper maché egg or yellow chicken.

His delicate fingers run through the fluffy fur of the grey bunny that's been displayed in my shop window every Easter I've owned the shop. The children love it and wave at it as they walk by on their way to and from school. In previous years, I've just scowled at them, but this year, something's different, and I just can't bring myself to do it. Scowl, that is. It's like I can't get my mouth to work properly. Oh God, now he's burying his button nose in the bunny's grey fur, sniffing it, eyelashes batting in clear delight.

"Mr Sable!" I spit a little louder than intended, his body jerking as the bunny flies over his shoulder, landing in a pile of cardboard boxes. His cheeks spill over into a bright scarlet like he's been caught in the act. If only. I'd die to see what he looks like when he touches himself, when he comes. I'd trade places with the bunny's ears between his fingers in a heartbeat. I'd—

"Yes, Mr Bennett, sir." He beams expectantly at me, his pale eyes darkening. I'm not going to call him Bunny. I'm not going to call him...

"Mr Sable, can I see you in the back, please?" I grit.

"But what about the—" He points to the half-finished window.

"Leave it!"

"Yes, Mr Bennet, sir," he obeys, instantly jumping from the stool, causing it to wobble, then tip over, landing on its side with a loud crash. He looks up, mortified, colour draining from his face.

"Leave it," I sigh, starting for the back of the shop. Aside from Benjamin's clumsiness, he's every shopkeeper's wet dream for a shop assistant. He's never late, and he's at my beck and call within seconds. My cock swells in my pants at the image of Benjamin on his knees for me, begging for me to stuff my length down his throat, squashing that *Master* before he can speak it. The light *tap-tap-tap* of his boots on the hardwood floor tells me he's following me like a good little pet—No! There'll be none of that. *Be professional, Easter. Be professional.*

Once in the back, I turn around, only to find him shifting on his feet in front of me, wringing his hands as he looks at me expectantly.

"I have a special task for you, Mr Sable." He nods eagerly, bouncing on his feet like a kid on Christmas Day.

"Yes, Mr Bennett, sir." He smiles carefully. "Anything you want." *Anything you want.* Fuck my pathetic life, but I want to hold him to that so badly, you have no idea. Looking frantically around the storage room, I find myself grasping at straws, my mind going completely blank, ignoring the real reason I brought him here. Then my gaze lands on the large cardboard box under the table to the left. Bingo!

"I need you to organise the chocolate moulds and catalogue them. I need to know the exact amount of every type of mould in preparation for the holidays. We'll be busy, and I need to be organised." Never has bullshit left my mouth this quickly. I put the goddamn O in organised. There isn't a single thing in this shop that I don't know by heart, inside and out. Benjamin doesn't seem to notice, though. Pulling a small pink notepad with an attached pen from his back pocket, he starts taking down notes, the tip of his tongue doing things to his bottom lip that should be illegal in his Majesty's kingdom. He nods attentively as I speak, his grey-brown eyes moving between the notepad and my lips. "You'll find a reference sheet in the cabinet that you'll be able to match the moul—"

"I know them!" he blurts, blushing, and I want to just lick along his cheek and chin to find out if the red tastes as good as it looks. Like ripe raspberries and all things lush and dirty.

"What do you mean, you know them?"

"I...I took the liberty of studying the sheet yesterday afternoon." He swallows audibly. "It was after I finished cleaning up the kitchen. I swear, I was done..." he trails off, mumbling something, eyes downcast.

"What was that?" I ask. "And will you please look at me, Mr Sable, when I talk to you?" Looking back up, his eyes are moist and I'm seconds away from asking him to get down on his knees for me again or sweeping him into my arms and carrying him upstairs, cradling him against my chest. I can't decide on which, to be honest; both options are equally tempting.

"Sorry, Mr Bennett, sir," he whispers. "I just...I wanted to be prepared, so I studied the sheet to save time.

I…I…" My brain does that weird thing again where I'm supposed to say and do something, only I've forgotten it and a different Easter—perhaps the real Easter, I'm not sure—speaks instead.

"I got you something," I grunt, like I'm already regretting it. He perks up instantly, so I quickly add, "Don't get too excited now. It's just something to wear as part of your Easter uniform." It's not. I'm lying through my teeth. I'm so full of it. This is not fucking *Disneyland*; there's no Easter costume. But Benjamin doesn't know that, and the way he looks at me, almost like I've just told him his monthly salary is, in fact, a million quid paid in pure gold, I'm not the least bit sorry that I've just pulled an Easter uniform out of my arse.

"What is it?" he breathes, twirling the pink pen between his fingers, his grey-brown gaze coasting around the room. My heart does a ridiculous somersault in my chest at the sheer anticipation in his eyes, his voice dripping with intrigue. I don't recall ever having been the cause of someone looking this… *elated*. It's quite the power rush, really. One could get used to it. Turning around, I reach for the top shelf where I put the small box that was delivered this morning. Two nights ago, I finally caved after a serial wanking session, images of Benjamin fondling that damn toy bunny burned into my retinas, the word *Bunny* on repeat in my deranged, over-sexed mind. You'd be surprised what you can get from *Amazon* when you type in the word 'Bunny.' Express delivery, too, for those of us who are impatient bastards, just barely hanging on to our sanity.

Placing the box on the large worktable, I nod, trying to get a grip on myself and control my voice. "Open it." He nods obediently, returning the notepad and pen to his back pocket. Never have I wanted anything more than to be that hand. His slim, pale fingers reach for the box, a look of awe painted on his beautiful face. Excruciatingly slowly, he starts peeling at the tape, my fucking heart in my throat, blood pounding in my ears. He'll probably think I'm mad. Oh shit, perhaps I've gone mad. What was I thinking? I blame Sir Cums-a-Lot, who's currently throbbing in my pants. He's led me astray. He'll eventually be the end of me.

Finally, *fucking finally*, Benjamin has managed to peel off the tape, some of it now stuck to his shirt. He smiles at me apologetically.

"Go on," I grunt. "We don't have all day."

"Yes, Mr Bennett, sir." Oh, for shit's sake, just kill me now. Just fucking kill me already. The tips of his fingers slide beneath the lid of the box as he carefully flicks it open. White silk paper appears, and he looks at me questioningly. I nod again, my voice caught in my throat. As he pulls the paper aside, something pale pink and fluffy appears. Oh shit, they are so pink. And fluffy. And just...

"I think I got the wrong—" I blurt, trying to backpedal just as Benjamin exhales a long sob, followed by an ear-piercing squeal. Pulling the bunny ears from the box, he takes them in like they're the holy fucking grail and not a ridiculous *Made in China* accessory. With a muffled whimper, he tugs them against his chest, tears brimming in his eyes as he looks at me; a world of gratitude and... adoration in them. Pure, unadulterated adoration. No one has ever looked at me like that. Never. I am not an adorable man. I'm not.

"Can...can I...are these for me?" His lofty *me* rings through the room, his huge eyes staring right into my very soul. My poor, deranged soul. He brushes at the fluffy ears as he bites into his plump bottom lip. "Can I put them on?" he whispers, staring directly at me, seeing right through me. Easter uniform, my arse. I bite out a raspy, "Yes," while my mind goes to all sorts of dangerous places. Fluffy bunny tails. Pink jumpsuits and pink stockings. See-through negligees. Silky-soft and feathery beneath my fingers. Milky-white creamy skin clad in the most exquisite pink lace, a bunny tail sticking out from...

"How do I look?" Benjamin blushes, bouncing on his feet, his rich chocolate-coloured hair framed by the headband, the pink bunny ears flip-flopping temptingly as he moves. "Is it okay?" he falters in my silence. "Is it...is it how you imagined it would look, Mr Bennett, sir?"

Chapter Six

I think I broke my boss. Any minute now I expect his head to start spinning in true Exorcist style and for smoke to come out of his ears. His usually clear blue eyes have turned a dark and ominous midnight blue, the black pupils dilated, his nostrils flaring slightly. His well-kept blond hairstyle is threatening to spill onto his frowning forehead, the golden bangs just waiting to cascade into his eyes. He looks positively feral and the bunny in me shivers because don't we all have a deeply hidden fantasy about being captured and consumed by the big bad wolf? But before I can bare my neck in defeat or hump Mr Bennett's thigh—whichever comes first—he blurts out a strangled "Excuse me," turns on his heel and disappears out the side door to the upstairs flat.

Bummer. Just when I thought he was going to call me Bunny again. I saw it right there on the tip of his tongue when it swept along his bottom lip. Those two elusive syllables now haunt me night and day. *Bun-ny*. I could've sworn he was going to call me that again. Perhaps even a growly, breathy version of it. *Oh, Bunny. My Bunny. Bunny, bunny, bunny*. But alas, no, just a tortured *excuse me*. And now that I'm alone, I feel so silly and pathetic for pining over my boss. The bunny ears must feel it, too, because they simultaneously decide to flop into my forehead in an explicit bow of defeat. What was I thinking? This is just a uniform, as Mr Bennett told me, and not a continuation of what happened the other day; what I've been referring to as '*The day Bunny got a Master.*' Crap.

A loud crash from upstairs followed by a muffled '*bollocks*' startles me, making me jump, the bunny ears tumbling off my head in a final surrender. Everything is quiet again, just the usual hum of cars and conversation from the street outside seeping through the windows. Bending, I pick up the bunny ears and place them carefully back in the box with an outdrawn sigh. Better get back to work or Mr Bennett will for sure—if he hasn't already decided to—fire my sorry arse.

I spend the next half an hour sorting out the storage room, which is already very neat and organised. My gaze continues to drift towards the box with the bunny ears, and every time my eyes catch the flimsy fluffy pink material, it sends a piercing pain through my heart. Perhaps it's truly time to grow up and let go of this childish dream of being Bunny? Maybe my parents were right all along that I'm not cut out for this world, that I'm a useless dreamer and I need to pull my head out of fantasy land and grow up? Perhaps I need to once and for all let go of my deep-seated longing of one day finding my Master? Maybe he isn't even out there. Although... it did feel so very real the other day when I crawled for him, and he called me... *that*.

When I'm happy with the back, I move into the front of the store. It's closed for customers since it's Sunday and I just came in to finish the window display. Everything is so quiet you could hear a pin drop, just the occasional crack of a floorboard from upstairs when Mr Bennett moves around. I wonder what he's doing? Perhaps he's preparing my letter of termination, although I haven't even received my work contract yet. Perhaps he's contemplating calling animal control to have the rabid rabbit evicted from his shop? Thank God I took off the bunny ears.

Once I've finished decorating the large window—it takes me absolutely no time now that Mr Bennett isn't here to distract me with his broad shoulders and looming gaze—I look around the deserted shop, shadows from the streetlights outside moving along the walls. I have no idea what time it is, only that it turned dark while I was working. I've never been good with time; just aware that it's either daylight, twilight, or nighttime. Mr Bennett usually tells me when to go home in that gruff voice of his that sends shivers down my spine and flames licking up my loins.

'You're dismissed, Mr Sable,' he will usually grunt, avoiding eye contact. Every time I feel like leaping, floating, flying into his arms, murmuring, 'Yes, please, Mr Bennett, sir. Please dismiss me!' I don't know why, but I just get so very, very wet when he tells me that.

So now I just stand here helplessly, looking at the door like the handle is going to bite me, wondering what I should do. Should I just leave? Would that be rude? I don't know. I've never been good with social cues. What does one do when one's boss stormed off after seeing one wearing gifted bunny ears? I have no idea, and I doubt there's even a manual or a Wikipedia page for this epic conundrum.

On a whim, I decide to go check on Mr Bennett before I leave because what if he isn't okay? It's been quiet for a long time, and what if he really did have a bunny-ear-induced stroke? Oh God, what if Mr Bennett is waiting for me to do CPR or give him the kiss of life? I'm hoping for the latter, obviously, because right now, I can't for the life of me recall what the C-P-R stands for.

Throwing my coat on the counter, I walk slowly towards the stairs to the upstairs flat. Licking my lips, I exhale deeply, before I call out, "Mr Bennett, sir?" Nothing. The shop remains eerily quiet; no squeaking floorboards above me or muffled *bollocks*. Crapio. Perhaps there's the odd chance that Mr Bennett decided to take an afternoon nap, although he doesn't strike me as a spontaneous napper. Clearing my throat, I call out again, this time a little louder, "Mr Bennett, sir? I'm done for today, so if you don't need me, I'll go home?" *Please need me, please need me, please need me.* Again, nothing. Fluffing, fluffy fluff tail, I cannot have the early demise of my boss on my conscience. I haven't even been here a full month. This is not good.

On their own, my feet start moving up the stairs carefully, the steps creaking beneath me. Once I near the door to the flat, I can make out a soft *thump-thump-thump* that grows in volume with each step, its repetitive sound drawing me closer. Perhaps Mr Bennett is building something, although he doesn't strike me as a builder either. Or maybe he's trying to send me a desperate message for help? *May-day. May-day. May-day. Save me, Bunny. Save me.* The closer I get, the louder the frantic *thump-thump-thump* becomes. My mind runs rampant with all sorts of dreadful scenarios. Mr Bennett in the grasp of a horrible seizure, his head banging against the floor, white foam frothing around his mouth. Mr Bennett locked inside his bathroom, banging on the door as the water rises on the floor beneath his feet, threatening to pull him under.

In my desperate mind, I've become Mr Bennett's saviour. This is my time to shine. This is my one and only opportunity to prove myself to Mr Bennett. Pushing at the door with my hand, it doesn't move. I reach for the door handle, but the door is locked. Oh shit. The thump continues, increasing in volume and speed. I need to get to him. My master needs me. My heart pounds in my chest, mingling with the desperate pounding sound.

"Do not fear, Mr Bennett!" I call out as I start pushing at the door. But it's solid as a rock, unmoving, and my arms are so stupidly frail and thin anyway that it's not surprising at all. Another sound erupts in between the thumps. A desperate groan, perhaps Mr Bennett's final battle against the claws of an untimely death. I can't have it. I can't have my master taken from me now that I've finally found him. In one final attempt to get to him, I decide to throw myself against the door, pain shooting up my shoulder as it connects with the solid wood. But I do not falter. This is not the time. The groaning has become a whine by now, the thumping has stopped and I fear I'm too late.

"Mr Bennett," I sob against the door as I give it another heavy push. This time, something shifts, and the door moves slightly. And suddenly I'm no longer Benjamin, useless and pathetic. A strength of unparalleled proportions grows inside me and I'm the Duke of Wellington himself. This is it. The door is my Waterloo. Mr Bennett is my Europe. The entire Seventh Battalion is behind me, cheering me on. *Bunny! Bunny! Bunny!* I must save him.

In a final display of strength I didn't think I possessed, I burst through the door, nearly bringing it with me. Desperate, I look down the hallway; still no sight of Mr Bennett. I perk my bunny ears, sniffing deeply, until a pitiful whimper drifts towards me from a closed door at the end of the hall. Thank God! I'm not too late!

"Master!" I call out. "Do not despair! Your Bunny is coming for you!" I run hastily down the hallway, decorum flying out the window, as I blow through the door. I'm panting, my eyes drifting across the room in a desperate search for my master. And there he is, displayed on his bed, a white-knuckled fist wrapped around something throbbing, angry-looking and very, *very* hard. And red. Ruby red. Creamy, milky-white liquid is oozing from the red, cascading down his fingers, and there is even some smeared across his golden abdomen because, of course, my master's skin is like pure gold, too. His naked chest is heaving, his stomach muscles clenching and unclenching, rippling like a stormy sea of angry waves. His mouth is twisted into a pained sigh, his usually contained facial features distorted. Sweat beads across his forehead and his eyes are squeezed tight.

He's beautiful. Just beautiful. I always knew he would be beautiful when he comes. As he opens his lips, a desperate sound wafts towards me. "Bunny." My heart soars in my chest. I wasn't wrong. I didn't imagine it. I am not useless or pathetic. I'm powerful. I'm the master of my master, it seems.

"Yes, Master," I answer his call, taking a step towards him, his heady, musky scent hitting my nostrils, my mouth salivating. "I'm here." As if waking up from the deepest of dreams, or perhaps electrocuted, Mr Bennett's eyes fly open, his blue eyes fiery and wild.

Chapter Seven

"Benjamin?" I blink once, twice, still engulfed in the aftermath of my powerful and third orgasm of the day. At first, I think I'm dreaming. That my filthy, oversexed mind has conjured him from the depths of my depraved soul. Then slowly, the daze lifts and that ever-present '*Mr Bennett, sir*' drifts towards me. My gaze connects with his muddy-grey eyes, spilling over with... *worry* before it turns into relief, I think.

"What the hell!" I shout, springing from my bed as I struggle with my pants that are acting as a homemade booby trap around my ankles. I nearly stumble into the nightstand, my sticky hand sliding against the corner when I try to steady myself. Right, cum hands. Classy. Benjamin comes charging at me, his eyes wild as he sweeps up a box of tissues from my dresser, pulling sheets frantically from the opening. Throwing them at me like rice at a wedding, a pink blush creeping across his cheeks as he starts mumbling something.

"What?!" I spit, catching a tissue as it comes flying at me. He winces, pearly teeth digging into his trembling bottom lip, and I instantly curse myself. "Sorry," I try, as I start wiping cum from my stomach, my limp dick hanging between my thighs in a resigned *'was this the blissful aftermath I was promised?'* slump. Yes, yes, I fear this was it. Crumbling the messy tissues in my hands, I look around for a place to discard them, but I come up blank. Where, oh where, does one discard cum stained tissues in front of one's only employee? I swear you can't make this shit up. You can't.

"You're okay," he pants, his voice tinged with surprised relief.

"Of course, I'm okay! Why wouldn't I be?" He shrugs, then nods at my hand.

"Give them to me," he whispers, his voice frail and shaky. He reaches out his hand between us, palm open, and for some strange reason—that I'll have to think really hard about later, but not now when my dick is still hanging out—I drop them into his hand. Closing his fingers around the sticky tissues, his gaze drops to the floor, while I bend to pull my pants up, adjusting myself. This is far from ideal. This is the opposite of ideal. This is... *undeal.* Benjamin is a stellar employee, and I doubt I'll find anyone as dedicated and skilled before the holidays, if ever. Then again, how do you move on from your employee—your *only* employee—seeing your dick? Seeing your dishevelled self in a post-orgasmic state with *his* name on *your* lips. That's a hard one, no pun intended.

"Mr Sable," I grunt, almost brushing a hand through my chaotic hair before I catch myself. I'm not convinced they're completely cum free. "We need to talk."

He looks up, a glimmer of hope flashing in his eyes as he bounces slightly on his feet.

"Yes, Mr Bennett, sir," he quips.

"About boundaries. *Personal* boundaries," I clarify, and the light instantly dims in his eyes.

"Oh..." he breathes.

"Look, Mr Sable, this isn't going to work, I'm afraid." It isn't. Not in a million years. So why do the words feel like acid on my tongue as I speak them? Why does it feel like my gut is about to drop out of my arse? Like my heart is trying to eat itself in a fit of... *something.* He tilts his head, his fawn eyes filling with tears, that full bottom lip trembling ominously. Then he does something that has been a fixed part of every sex fantasy of mine since he did it the first time downstairs. He drops to his knees.

"Please don't fire me, Mr Bennett, sir," he whispers, a sob lingering at the end. Oh shit. "Please, please, please, Mr Bennett, s—" The rest of the 'sir' is swallowed by the saddest hiccup in history. Oh, for Christ's sake. My stomach does a weird flip, and I swallow back a groan. Be professional, Easter. Be professional.

"Please get up, Mr Sable," I bite out, but he just shakes his head furiously at me, brown locks spilling onto his forehead and into his teary eyes. His cheeks are wet, and I feel like pulling him from the floor and tugging him against my chest to shut up my traitorous heart. My dick seems to be on board with that idea because he perks up while the image of Benjamin wearing those damn bunny ears flashes through my mind.

"Please, please, please," he chants, his gaze locking onto mine as fat tears spill down his cheeks and further down his chin and neck. "I thought you were in danger!" he blurts, his voice filled with genuine alarm, indignation blazing in his eyes. "I thought..."

"Danger?" I ask. "Why on earth did you think I was in danger?"

"Because," he gulps, scrambling towards me on his knees until he's right at my socked feet. "Because of the noise," he whispers, licking his lips, his trembling fingers reaching for the hem of my pants.

"The noise?" I sigh, pinching the top of my nose, cum fingers be damned. He nods eagerly as his fingers squeeze around my woollen pants like I'm the last straw during a raging storm. And then he tells me. His account makes little sense at first as the words spill from his lips. Something about Waterloo and the Seventh Battalion. How he can't remember what C-P-R stands for and that it sounded like I was dying, choking, drowning. When he's done, he's panting at my feet, and I have to admit that somehow I do see how he could think that I was... *unwell*... for lack of a better word.

He looks at me expectantly, tears glistening on the tips of his dark lashes. Something shifts inside me then, a softness building in my chest as it slowly spreads to the rest of my body. Until it has invaded every limb and every vessel. Every cell. Until I can't stand it any longer—not a damn second longer—my body aching, needing, calling out for him. *Bunny. My Bunny.* He thought I was in danger. He wanted to save me. He... he *cares* about me. It's evident in his eyes, in his words, in the submissive way he kneels at my feet, clinging desperately to my pants, that dirty tissue still clenched in his other small fist.

"Come here," I rasp, giving in, because the alternative is unbearable. Who am I kidding, really? Scrambling from the floor and into a standing position, he sways on his feet, his fingers reaching for my chest, the tissue dropping to the floor. His wet eyelashes flutter, an unspoken plea hidden in the depths of his eyes. Wrapping my arms around him, he's small and frail, quivering against my chest. I lift him easily off the floor, cradling him against me. His thighs widen on instinct as he lets me hold him, his slender legs locking around my waist. He weighs next to nothing. He's like a shivering baby animal in my arms. My Bunny.

A broken sigh leaves his body as he buries his face against my neck, sniffing audibly.

"I'm so sorry," he whimpers, his hands finding my neck, blunt nails digging into my skin, gliding through my hair, pulling at the strands. "I really did think that—"

"There, there," I speak against the top of his head, the sweetness of his scent filling my lungs. I allow myself to breathe him in as I continue to comfort and reassure him that everything is truly fine. Because it is, isn't it? For the first time in a long while, I feel calm, no longer at war with myself and the world. The storm has passed and holding my Bunny against me feels like walking out from a dark cave and into the brightness of the daylight. Scary, yet strangely freeing too.

He sniffles against my left ear, then sighs as he exhales languidly. I press another kiss against the crown of his head and he giggles softly as the tip of his tongue sneaks out and licks my earlobe. I laugh then. I can't help it. I can't help myself. I don't *want* to help myself.

"You're laughing," he murmurs against my ear, his voice filled with wonder, and I can feel the smile on his lips. My chest puffs out. I decide then and there that I love his smile. It's mine now. "I didn't think you could," he teases. "I thought you were from before laughter was invented."

"Hey, I'm not that old, you little pest." My fingers dig into his sides and I pinch him gently. He squirms and I adjust him in my arms.

"You can put me down now," he breathes. The hell I can, and I tell him exactly just that.

"I'm never putting you down," I grunt, squeezing him tighter against me, a left-over sob leaving his lips.

"Ne-ver?" he stammers, a world of hope in those two syllables. "Not even when you have to go...you know..." he giggles, his voice breathy and happy.

"Well, perhaps then," I admit, a strange sensation of regret and loss running through my body at the thought of putting him down. There's a moment of silence between us before he speaks again.

"Master?" The word hangs in the air around us, doing things to my insides like it did the last time, giving me purpose, giving me life.

"Yes, Bunny," my voice comes out muffled by his hair.

"There is no Easter uniform, is there?" His voice is frail and vulnerable, his fingers digging into my sweater. I shake my head. "Those bunny ears were for me, weren't they? Just for me?" I nod, swallowing, willing my tongue to function.

"They were. They *are*," I say and then, because we already reached the point of no return when he saw me come with his name—*my* name for him—on my lips and then decided carrying my only employee in my arms was a good idea, I add, "Do you want to see the rest?"

His head whips back from my neck, his eyes wide open, his mouth slightly agape.

"There's more?" he gasps, his eyes filling again, an ocean of muddy grey swimming before me. I laugh again, this time heartily and deeply. Uninhibited and carefree like I used to be in a faraway past... before I turned into a broody bastard.

"Of course, there's more. So much more." Like I said, the number of hits you get when you search for *bunny* on Amazon...

Chapter Eight

I'm convinced I must have gone to Bunny Heaven or something just like it. That when I entered Mr Bennett's flat, bursting through his door, it was instead a portal to an alternate universe. Some weird rabbit's hole sucking me into a world I hardly recognise. Mr Bennett is different too. After the initial shock of seeing me in the door to his bedroom, he hasn't stopped smiling, nor has he stopped touching me. Petting me, actually. His usually cool blue eyes are warm and tender when he looks at me, his voice deep and gentle when he calls me by my name. *Bunny.*

"How did you know?" I ask, my voice filled with awe as I take in the accessories displayed on Mr Bennett's sage-green duvet. I eventually convinced him it was okay for him to put me back down for now. I told him he could always sweep me back up into his strong arms whenever the urge to hold me or carry me strikes. He looked at me doubtfully, grunting something unintelligible, until I grasped his cheeks in my hands, cradling them carefully, while my eyes found his.

'*I'm not going anywhere,*' I reassured him, and the wolf inside him seemed to relax, comforted by my words.

My gaze glides from a pink furry bunny tail to what I think are wristbands made of snowy white fake fur. My fingers itch to put them on, but I try to contain myself because I have a feeling that Mr Bennett wants to dress me. He looks up from the black delivery box, tilting his head at me, something silky and lacy clasped in his hands. A wondrous frown dwells between his dark blond brows.

"I didn't," he says softly, answering my question, the tanned skin around his eyes crinkling as he takes me in. I shiver. I could get used to this version of Mr Bennett way too easily. The newfound softness in his voice and the tenderness in his eyes when he looks at me. His smile. His laughter. Like rare gemstones. "I hoped..." he trails off, shrugging slightly, as he pulls the delicate fabric from the box. He lets out a long, shaky exhale as he unfolds the garment. "When I saw you touching the bunny while you were doing the window display, there was such..." he sucks in a breath. "There was such longing in your eyes. Like you... like you were jealous of that toy bunny."

"I was," I say, smiling at him. He nods slowly, solemnly holding out the garment between us.

"This is for you," he says a little gruffly. "I mean...if you like it, that is. If you are...you know...inclined towards such...*things.*" And then he goes and does something that I never expected. He blushes. Mr Bennett blushes like a shy schoolboy. He's adorable. He's so... prim and proper. So well-articulated and almost rigid in his posture and his mannerisms. But I know he's in there, hiding in the shadows. My wolf. My big, bad, hungry wolf. God, I can't wait to ruffle his fur and lure him out. I know he wants to. It's only a matter of time.

"I am," I say, my voice steady as a beat. Sucking my bottom lip into my mouth, I take in the satin fabric. It's a dusty pink, *tea rose*, if I'm not mistaken, with white lace trimmings and tiny silk bows from the neckline and all the way down the front of the... jumpsuit? It's not exactly a jumpsuit, is it? More like underwear. A one-piece. The bottom part is similar to a pair of sleep shorts and has lace trimmings, too. "It's lovely," I breathe, my heart expanding in my chest. "It's very lovely," I gulp, my fingers reaching for the shimmery fabric.

Mr Bennett's entire face lights up, sunshine in his eyes, his golden skin glowing. "Yeah?" he asks, his voice filled with vulnerability and longing.

"Yes," I smile at him. "I always dreamed of having something this...*delicate*," I say. I run my fingers along the front of the one-piece, curling the tips around one of the tiny bows. He puffs out his chest with pride at my praise, a smile growing from the corner of his mouth. God, Mr Bennett is so sexy when he smiles. He truly is. Like real movie star sexy. But not those clean-cut contemporary actors. No, not them. More like Cary Grant or Montgomery Cliff or Rock Hudson. That unorthodox male beauty. Or Robert Redford with that golden head of hair of his and intense gaze. Those quiet, brooding types; when they finally smile, it lights up the entire universe.

"You haven't even seen the back yet," he blurts, his eyes eager.

"Show me then." I smile at him with newfound confidence, my gaze connecting with his and I swear sparks fly all around us, the air electric. He nods, then turns the piece around by the spaghetti shoulder straps. And I almost swoon at the sight, my dick perking up in my slacks. There are tiny ivory-white buttons running all the way down the back, like a trail leading all the way down to where the shorts begin. But they don't stop there. The back of the shorts has small buttons that go all the way down, too. Way, *way* down.

"It's so that...you know...I thought it would look nice when you wear the tail," he murmurs, his warm breath hitting my chin. A squeal leaves my mouth on its own accord as I leap into his arms. He scrambles to catch me as I dive straight for his neck, burying my face against his clean-shaven chin, breathing him in, the scent of bitter cocoa and oranges engulfing me.

"I love it!" I sniff against his neck. "Thank you, thank you, thank you, Mr Bennett, sir!" A low, satisfied rumble grows in his chest until it leaves his lips as a loud laugh. Holding me out in front of him, he searches my face.

"You're a funny little thing, aren't you?" he muses. "So...so impulsive and...and altogether remarkable." He holds me tighter in his grasp.

"Remarkable? Me?" No one has ever referred to me as remarkable before, on the contrary. I've been called many things throughout my nearly twenty-four years on this planet, but remarkable has never been one of them. "You think I'm remarkable?" I whisper.

"I do." He nods, his expression turning serious. "Are you sure you like it? I mean, you don't have to wear it just because—" The rest of his words are swallowed up by my lips as I press them firmly against his. I've never kissed anyone before and I'm not sure if I'm doing it correctly. At least not until he starts kissing me back, a deep, contented hum emanating from his mouth. Ever so slowly, his lips part, his warm breath ghosting along my lips as he sucks my bottom lip into his mouth, suckling it. There's nothing hungry about the kiss, although I can feel him getting hard as I rub my crotch against his. It's careful and tentative and while I've never made love to anyone, it rather feels like he's making love to my mouth. The taste of him explodes on my tongue, and for a couple of seconds, it feels like I'm floating or losing consciousness, or perhaps even both. Then his lips are gone, his lips, and with my eyes closed, I chase them blindly, already addicted to him, my master.

"Wow," I breathe, my lips tingling, my chest filled with a thousand robins. "That was...that was..." As I open my eyes, I'm met by the deepest, darkest blue I've ever seen, the colour nearly stealing the air from my lungs. He suddenly looks shy, my Mr Bennett. Hesitant. "Does that answer your question?" I say.

"My question?" He regards me, puzzled like he, too, has had all the air knocked out of him.

"Whether I like it."

"Maybe?" he swallows, smiling at me.

"It's perfect," I say, sweeping a lock of his blond hair out of his eyes. "Just like you, Mr Bennett." He exhales deeply, his eyes shifting between my eyes and my lips. They burn from his piercing gaze. *I* burn from his gaze.

"No more 'Mr Bennett'," he says pointedly. "I think we are way past that point in our relationship; wouldn't you agree, Bunny?" I nearly drop my jaw, my mind fixating on that one word. *Relationship.* "You can call me Easter or—"

"Master?" I cut him off before mumbling an apology, digging my front teeth into my bottom lip.

"Yes, you can call me Master, too, but perhaps not when other people are around." He raises an eyebrow at me in warning and I nod compliantly.

"Can I call you East?" I ask, my entire body buzzing with the last remnants of energy I can muster. What a day, huh?

"Yes," he chuckles. "You can call me East too."

"Okay. East it is then, Master," I grin at him, a strange tiredness pulling at my limbs, as I try to suppress a yawn. Worried eyes are on me in a heartbeat.

"My poor darling," he rasps. "You worked so hard today. And then you saved me, too." There's a wet sheen to his eyes as he takes me in.

"I did save you, didn't I, Master?"

"You did, Bunny. You have no idea." His voice is shaky as he leans in and presses a chaste kiss against first my forehead, then the tip of my nose and finally my lips. It's just the softest of kisses, featherlight and barely there. Only it is there, right there, my second kiss ever. I could get used to this. I truly could. I sigh against his lips as I close my eyes, leaning into him.

"Let's get you fed, bathed, and then off to bed," he says. "It's way past your bedtime, my darling Bunny." And I just nod because everything he just said sounds like heaven. It does. I can't spend the night, obviously. I can't risk it. Not with him. Not with my master. Although *it* hasn't happened in a while, I know it *can* happen. It *has* happened. And that would be just horrendous. That would mean the end of this before it has even truly begun. So I can't. But I can stay for a little, pretending it's for good, and then when my master is asleep, I'll sneak out. I guess the garden can wait. The carrots aren't going anywhere, neither are the onions unless they suddenly decide to sprout a pair of legs. I giggle at that. "What?" he says, laughing too, brushing his thumb along my chin.

"Nothing," I grin. "Nothing at all, East. It sounds like heaven, is all."

Chapter Nine

I can't believe he's still here. That I haven't scared him off yet. First, with my chronic grumpiness—yes, we grumps are, in fact, aware we're grumpier than the average population—and then with the aggressive jerk-off session he walked in on. As jittery, clumsy, and nervous as Benjamin can be in the shop or when I ask him a simple work-related question, is as calm and assertive he is now. Finding your boss with his cock in hand and cum all over the place could hardly be considered an everyday occurrence, and still, he seemed to be more concerned about my well-being than mortified. To be honest, I don't know what I was thinking. Storming off like that to relieve myself while he was still downstairs. I can only write it off as another momentary lapse of judgment, my instincts taking over, common sense and restraint flying out the window.

There was just something about him, *Bunny.* Seeing him wearing those bunny ears that *I*, East, bought for him on a whim. Because somewhere deep inside of me, there had been that urge to get them for him. And not just the ears, no. In a lust-induced shopping spree, I'd indulged in everything flimsy, fluffy, and pink on Amazon. For him. My Bunny. Because some part of me had hoped it was truly him. The one I'd been waiting for all my life.

I meant it when I told him he's a funny little thing. He is. Quite remarkable, like I also told him. Shit, I told him a lot of things, didn't I? As naturally submissive as he appears to be, there's also something confident and assertive about him as well. He didn't hesitate when I showed him my gifts, nor did he blink even once. It was almost as if he, too, knew it could only ever end up this way. The inevitability of our meeting. The indisputable connection from day one. The way he seems to recognise my deepest, darkest thoughts and desires before I'm even aware of them myself. I wonder if I do the same to him? Do I see him before he sees himself? Does he perhaps need me—like I need him, it seems—to truly be himself? I don't know. This is all so sudden, so new, although it feels like he was always mine. As much as I want to rush this thing between us, I know that I have to step on the brakes just a tad. I can't risk scaring him off. Not when I've finally found him.

On that note, where the hell is he? He was just going to the loo while I started the bath, but it's been what now? Five minutes, perhaps? I've finished drawing the bath, fragrant steam billowing from the soapy surface of the water. It wasn't until I reached for the bath foam that I realised I had no idea what scent he liked. I know so very little about him, and still, our souls seem to be ancient mates. So I decided on the orange blossom because although it's slightly sweet like him, it's tangy too. There's an edge to the sweetness just like there's an edge to my sweet, innocent Bunny. Sweeping the tips of my fingers through the water, I test the temperature.

Perfect. I know the warmth will leave his skin all pink and prickly, but it won't scald him.

After another minute or two, I can no longer stand it. A strange unease overtakes me, and I leave the bathroom and walk towards the toilet, only to find it empty. My chest tightens as my stomach drops. Shit, it was too much—I am too much—after all. I did manage to scare him away. Shit.

"East?" Oh, thank God. Thank the good old fucking Lord. I think I turn around so fast that I get a whiplash but who cares? He takes me in all wide-eyed and flushed as he nibbles on his bottom lip.

"I thought you'd gone!" I blurt as I rush towards him, closing the gap between us. "I thought..." I grit as I haul him back into my arms, up against my chest, right where he belongs. A succession of small whimpers escapes him as I squeeze him tighter against me, breathing him in. Sighing against my chest, he goes all soft and pliant in my arms, melting into me, his slender arms snaking around my waist.

"I was thirsty," he murmurs. "I just went to get some water." Then he chuckles, "I'm right here, East. I told you already. I'm not going anywhere. Not unless you want me to."

"I don't!" I blurt, burying my face in his dark curls. "I don't," I repeat, swallowing behind the lump building in my throat while words like *always* and *forever* and *mine* tumble through my head. Inhaling deeply, I try to collect myself. Resurfacing from his fragrant locks, I push him away from me slightly, clasping his face in my palms. He looks at me with adoration—yes, there's no mistake about that—in his muddy grey eyes. Sucking in another breath, I nearly lose myself in the vastness of his gaze, two dark orbits threatening to suck me in, swallow me up and spin me right out of control. Then he blinks as he whispers, "East." Fuuuck, my name on his lips. It's everything, and my cock seems to recognise the massiveness of it too, because it hardens in my pants.

"Your bath's ready," I croak before I lean in and press a light kiss against his nose. "Nice and warm and foamy." He nods carefully, a flash of heat sparking in his eyes. "Come," I say, releasing my hands from his cheeks. Reaching for his left hand, I tangle my fingers through his and pull him after me towards the bathroom, the scent of orange blossom and sweet promises engulfing us as we get closer.

"I haven't had a real bath in ages," he whispers in awe as he takes in my large white bathtub. It's vitreous China-coated ceramic, giving it a glossy look. I had it installed when I re-did the entire flat above the shop. I rarely use it myself—I'm more of a quick in and out of the shower kind of guy, but now, as I take in Benjamin's glowing face, I know exactly why I got it. I got it for *him*. To pamper him. To take care of him. To make him feel *special*.

He turns, looking at me, an unspoken question lingering in his eyes. But it's like I hold the manual. The Benjamin B. Sable manual. The *How-to-take-care-of-your-Bunny* guide.

"You can have a bath whenever you want. Now, arms up." I smile as I take a step towards him. He obediently lifts his arms above his head, and I carefully grab the hem of his blue shirt. Sliding it up his body, flawless, creamy skin is revealed like the promised land, unmarked and pristine. *Mine*, my heart echoes, and my fingers itch to just tear off his clothes and devour him. But I can't. Not yet.

He giggles when the tips of my fingers brush along his skin and again when the shirt gets caught in his chocolate curls. He giggles, too, when a string of curses leaves my mouth as I battle his belt and wiggle the zipper in his pants. Every time his melodic, featherlight voice fills the room, it's like he invades my body, my soul, my entire being, and claims me in ways I never thought possible.

And then he stands before me in the smallest pair of sky-blue briefs, his hairless thighs slender and vibrating beneath my touch. I swallow as I take him in, on my knees for him. Sitting back on my heels, I reach for his right foot and place it on my left thigh. He sways for a brief moment, then catches his balance by burying his hands in my hair. My scalp tingles from his touch, every nerve ending buzzing as I focus on his small foot on my thick thigh. I frown as I take in the worn black sock. It's too plain and dull for my Bunny. I make a note to buy him new socks, packs of them, in all the pastel colours I can think of; sky blue, lemon yellow, pale pink, powdery purple, a—

"East?"

"Yeah?" I rasp, resurfacing from my newfound appreciation of pastel colours.

"Are you okay?" he asks hesitantly, his fingers lingering in my hair.

"Of course." I tilt my head up at him, smiling reassuringly. "I just...your socks are worn," I blurt, decorum flying out the window.

"I know," he says as I slide it off his foot. "I didn't expect anyone to see them today. Otherwise, I would've worn my nice pair." *My nice pair.* A wave of unprecedented anger rises inside me. *My nice pair.* If it were up to me, he'd only wear nice things from now on, in the finest, softest materials. Clothing that would caress his skin and treat it with the tenderness and comfort he deserves. I decide it's up to me, and the agitation in my chest clears somewhat.

When I've got rid of his socks—the left one revealing a large hole on the heel—I proceed to reach for his briefs, my eyes searching for his consent before I start tugging them down. He blushes shyly, then nods as his pearly white teeth dig into his plump bottom lip. His scent fills the air as I remove his briefs, a sweet muskiness invading my nostrils as he steps out of them. I'm seconds away from just burying my entire face in the dark curls surrounding his cock, but a low wince tears me from my trancelike state. Benjamin frowns at me, his eyes dark, and I realise my fingers are digging into the delicate skin of his thighs.

"Sorry," I rush out, releasing my grip on him, rubbing at the patches of skin that are now bruised a deep pink. "I'm sorry," I repeat. "I was too rough," I admit.

"East," he murmurs as he bends down, reaching for my hands. Linking his fingers through mine, he pulls me to my feet, his naked body such a contrast to my clothed one. He's so small and frail compared to my much larger frame, and I chastise myself for hurting him.

"I'll be more careful from now on," I mumble, my eyes drilling holes into the tiled floor beneath my feet. "I never want to hurt you."

"East, will you please look at me?" he says, squeezing my hands. "Please?"

I look up hesitantly, my gaze connecting with his.

"You didn't." He smiles at me, his eyes brimming with reassurance. "I'm just not used to..." He seems to search his mind for the next word. "I'm not used to being touched." He swallows. "It...it felt strange. Foreign. But nice," he adds. "I like it when you touch me. I like your hands on me, East. Don't ever be afraid of hurting me. You can't. Not you, East. Never you, my beautiful master."

Beautiful. The word pulls all the air from my lungs, and I think I lose consciousness for a moment. What is he doing to me, this... strange creature? It's like his mere presence turns me into a version of myself that I don't recognise. I feel stripped bare and vulnerable, but at the same time so immensely powerful. I wonder if my presence leaves him the same.

"Your bath is getting cold," I nod at the tub, steam still wafting from the surface.

"It's perfect." He smiles. "Thank you, Master." He blinks as I guide him into the steaming tub. A deep, guttural groan leaves his lips as the water meets his skin, swallowing his toes, his feet, and then his calves. I don't let go of him until he's completely submerged in the foamy water, his head leaning back on the edge of the tub that I've draped with the softest towel I own. He looks at me, pure bliss in his eyes, lashes fluttering in naked delight. I can make out the shape of him underneath the foam, but I can't see the individual features, and somehow, it's the single most erotic moment of my life.

"I'll order some food," I manage to say. "Then I'll be back to wash your hair." He moans at that image, his cheeks turning a fiery red as he closes his eyes. "Don't fall asleep now," I add, raising a brow at him in warning when he opens his eyes again.

"I won't, East," he says, his fingers trailing through the water, caressing the surface. And now I'm suddenly jealous of the water and tub holding him when my fingers itch to do the same. *Later*, I tell myself. Later I'll be the one to hold him, touch him, smell him. "I promise," he adds, and I can't help but hope and want, for the first time in maybe ever, that his promise means everything and anything. Because I want that. Everything and anything with him.

Chapter Ten

He washes every inch of my body with a soft sponge, leaving not a single spot untouched until I'm squeaky clean. He starts with my toes and he purses his lips into a semi-smile when I giggle. He's so handsome my eyes sting when I drink him in. Or at least, that's what I tell myself, but the real reason is his tenderness. It gets to me. The way he treats me like I'm something delicate and... and valuable. When he bends down and kisses each of my toes, I suck in a breath, in awe of his awe I guess. He continues up the front of my foot, pressing featherlight kisses as he moves towards my ankle. Then he pauses, murmuring something into my skin that I can't quite catch, but sparks a fire in his blue eyes when he looks up and his gaze connects with mine.

"Did you just whisper something to my ankle?" I chuckle.

"Yes," he swallows, the cerulean twin flames flickering at me.

"What was it?" I hold my breath.

"It's a secret," he says, bending back over my foot, sucking the skin into his mouth, laving at it with his tongue. I can't even be bothered to hold back the squeal that leaves my mouth—I'm enjoying this, whatever it is, way too much.

"What? You have secrets with my ankle now?" I pant. He nods, then moves up my lower leg, nipping at the skin. "Okay," I hum as I lean back in the warm, fragrant water, letting it soothe me while East worships my body—because I'm pretty sure that's what he's doing. Closing my eyes, I give in for the first time in my life. I hand over my power to him, my boss, my master, my East, because for some inexplicable reason, I trust him completely. And, aside from Mr Harvey, I've never trusted anyone before. The world has never given me much reason to, least of all, my own family.

Through a misty, orange-blossom haze, I register him lifting my right thigh, carefully sweeping the sponge along its back, then gently along my butt, caressing the crease, lingering there for a few seconds. The air around us becomes heady, almost sizzling, as he strokes the sponge along my crease before continuing to the other side, brushing across my butt cheek, then trailing along my other thigh. He's quiet and meticulous, like when he works in the shop, pouring warm, velvety chocolate into moulds or decorating delicate pieces with a pair of tweezers. I've watched him, sometimes for hours I'm sure, when he enters this sort of trancelike state, creating magic with his hands, a sprinkle of almonds here, a dusting of dry-frozen raspberries there. It's quite enchanting. Because he does have magical hands, bringing my entire body to this special place right now where there is nothing but raw pleasure and sensation.

"Come," he hums, reaching out his hands for me, a tender smile playing along his lips. My arms feel heavy as lead when I lift them and he cradles his hands around my elbows, pulling me up. His cheeks are flushed a dark pink, drops of sweat beading along the ridge of his nose and across his forehead. His hair curls deliciously from the humidity in the room, and he somehow looks younger than his years. I can't help smiling as I catch a glimpse of a young East, wondering if he was less grumpy back then, his smiles given more freely.

"What's so funny?" he glares, squeezing the sponge above my chest, water cascading down my pecs, my ribs, my stomach.

"Nothing," I moan, the feel of him so close to me doing things to my insides that I've never felt before.

"Is that so?" he says, a playful edge to his voice. Then he leans in, pursing his lips as he blows at my left nipple, before sucking it into his mouth, tugging at it with his teeth.

"Oh God," I moan again, this time in a deep, guttural way that sounds filthy and needy. "East," I gasp. "What are you..." My mouth fails me, along with the rest of my body, as I give into his lips, his touch, to him, my master. The rest of the world bleeds away, the tiled walls of the bathroom, the tub, everything, until there's only him and endless pleasure.

From then on, everything becomes a blur, fragments of moments registering when he pulls me from the tub and dries me with a fluffy towel that smells of clean cotton and summer blossom fields. When I'm dry, my skin buzzing deliciously from the contrast between the hot bath and the cool air, he wraps me in a dry, even fluffier towel, lifts me up in his strong arms, and carries me down the hallway and into his bedroom. I've lost all track of time, but the room is cast in a dim light from two lamps on his nightstands, so I guess it's late. He's pulled the duvet aside, crisp white sheets beckoning at me to just fall into this strange world of warmth and comfort. The scent of him, a faint memory of his arousal, lingers in the room, stirring my own need for him.

"Darling," I think he whispers as he presses a kiss to my forehead, then the tip of my nose and finally my mouth. "Darling," he repeats against my lips, and this time, I know that my mind isn't playing cruel tricks on me. "My darling Bunny," he hums as he leans his right knee on the bed and places me down in the middle, arranging my head and my hair on the soft pillow. Then he frowns, a flicker of doubt and perhaps fear appearing in his eyes. There's an unspoken question on his face, a question that won't allow him to go any further until I give him my permission. But there's no doubt in my heart. Not a single shred.

"Please," I beg him, holding out my arms towards him, spreading my thighs for him. It's like my body works on its own, under his spell, succumbing to his powerful presence, inviting him in. His expression softens, his eyes once again darkening, as he, too, gives in to the inevitability of the moment. With his knee still resting on the bed, he begins to strip, unbuttoning each button of his shirt carefully. There's a mindfulness to even this mundane of things; his fingers untucking the hem from his grey trousers, then sliding the fabric down his broad shoulders and toned arms. I suck in a breath, desire pooling in my stomach as my dick swells between my thighs. A groan escapes him, and he hurries to discard the shirt and unbuckle his belt.

"Don't laugh," he warns before I even realise that I was about to. "It's all your fault," he grits, not a trace of annoyance in his voice.

"Is it?" I pipe up, my neediness knowing no bounds.

"Yes," he exhales, shaking his head while he slides down his pants, revealing inches and inches of golden skin adorned with soft-looking blond hair. "I'm not normally like this," he says as he gets rid of his pants, dropping them on top of his shirt.

"What are you like, then?" I tease, my hand sweeping across my belly and further down towards the sparse scattering of dark hair surrounding my dick.

"Bunny," he says, suddenly all vulnerable and naked in front of me. "Don't play with me," he rasps, his gaze trailing hungrily along my body, down to where my hand is teasing the soft hair. "You know what I'm like," he says matter-of-factly as he leans in over me, his arms resting on each side of my head, his breath coasting along my chin.

"I do," I agree. "But I don't think that's really you, East." There's a boldness rising inside me that grows with each gesture of kindness from him. With each fond word and warm smile, it grows and grows, bursting through my chest and out into the world. Bunny has never been bold before, but I have to admit, I like it. "It's how you want the world to perceive you, East. All serious and stoic and..." The word escapes me momentarily, his blue eyes and sweet breath distracting me.

"And what?" he asks, a frown digging into the skin between his brows. "And what, Bunny?"

"Untouchable," I blurt.

"Untouchable," he repeats, tasting the word on his tongue before nodding. "Yes," he admits. "Perhaps I am. Or was." Regret flashes through his eyes. "I don't want to be, though. At least not to you, my darling Bunny. Never to you."

"I know," I say, closing the gap between us, my lips brushing lightly against his. I can't help but wonder what made him so... closed off. And what it is I do that makes his walls come down. I'll have to ask him sometime when I'm not so horny. He sighs, his body relaxing, his weight pressing against me, and I feel his hardness against my thigh, once again igniting my desire for him. "Please," I whimper as he thrusts his tongue into my mouth, stealing all the air from my lungs. And then he, once again, takes over my entire world, my mind going blank, my senses betraying me. And I don't mind. I don't mind at all. I think I even say it out loud at one point because he chuckles against my neck while my fists are buried in his hair.

"You don't mind, huh?" he laughs, biting the words into my skin, sure to leave bruises. But I don't mind that either. I want there to be bruises. I want him to cover me in them so that when I wake in the morning and look at myself in the mirror, I'll know this was all real and not a dream.

"I don't," I gasp, my back swaying as I rise from the bed to meet his touch, to give him better access. "I don't mind at all, East. I don't."

"Funny," he grits, now against my collarbone... or is it my chest? It's like he's everywhere all at once, consuming me, devouring me, my body humming with lust.

"Funny," I giggle, although I have no idea what he means. "Funny."

"Yes," he licks down my sternum, his tongue raspy and wet. "Such a funny little thing, aren't you, Bunny? My Bunny."

I nod, my eyes stinging, the 'my Bunny' floating through me, while he buries his face against my stomach, blowing raspberries against my belly button. Again, he surprises me, pulling laughter from my lips, his silliness so unexpected. I squirm underneath him, my fingers digging into his shoulders as his teeth find the hair around my dick, tugging at it.

"Please," I near-sob, asking him for something that is so foreign to me but that I know I only ever want to experience with him, my master. "Please, Master." I push my hips from the bed wantonly, all decorum gone.

"You want my mouth on you, Bunny? Is that what you want?" He sucks the words into my skin, his warm breath wrapping around my needy dick; a promise of what's to come.

"Yes, please. God, yes," I beg him. "I want it. Please, Master. I want it all."

Chapter Eleven

I'm not usually a giver. Most often I'm on the receiving end, just taking and taking, usually oblivious to my partners' needs. Or so at least I've been told. But with him, with Bunny, it's different. I *want* to give. No, I *need* to. As I suck his hard cock into my mouth, his pleasure becomes the sole focus of my world. Everything else ceases to exist and there's only him, my new compulsion. My only vice.

The taste of him explodes on my tongue; his sweetness with a tangy aftertaste addicting from the first lick. I'm doomed, I realise, without a shadow of regret. There will never be anyone else, but I accept my fate with calm gratitude. I'll never need anyone else, that much is clear. But whether I'll be enough for him... only time will tell.

I greedily suck his entire length into my mouth, all the way back into my throat, and he moans loudly, his fingers pulling at my hair. Fuck, he's so into this, into me, and my chest just about explodes with pride. Because I'm the one doing this to him. I'm the source of such explicit and vivid pleasure. And it's new. And addicting.

I know I bring people pleasure with my chocolate. That I make them drool and moan and sometimes feel intoxicated. I know they speak of the '*Bennett Effect*' while they swoon, batting their eyelashes in mock ecstasy. And I do take pride in that, quite a bit actually. But this is different. This is not my creation—it's *me*. What *I'm* doing to him right now, to my Bunny, taking him apart. *I'm* taking him apart, lick by lick, suck after suck.

He squirms underneath me, his cock leaking into my mouth, arousal emanating from his crotch, his hole, his entire body. I can't wait to take him, to bury my entire face against his hole, torturing him with my tongue until he comes on my face. Fuck, I want him to explode on my face. But not today. Not yet.

"Please," he whimpers, as he thrusts into my mouth, hitting the back of my throat. "*Yeeesss*," he moans as I gag around his cockhead. "Yes." I lick along the back of his cock, my tongue registering every vein and curve on the way, how he pulses and how he feels, until I reach his flushed cockhead. I stay there, circling my tongue around and around and around until he's sobbing with need.

"Please, Master," he pants. "So close. I'm so close." His fingers tighten in my hair, the sting causing goosebumps to erupt across my shoulders and down my spine, my cock so hard it's bordering on painful.

"Not yet, darling." I blow at his cockhead, and he whines. Like an animal, he whines as he arches his back, tilting his hips to chase my mouth. Laughter bursts from my lips at the sight of him, at the effect I have on him. The neediness that I pull from his body with my mouth alone. My lips buzz from the feel of him, and I dive back in, digging the tip of my tongue into his slit, the precum coating it. He screams then, his entire being shaking, his hands now claws threatening to pull me apart, too. I drink him in, sucking hungrily at his cock like a famished man. And when it comes to my sweet, sweet Bunny, I fear I am and always will be—famished and insatiable. "Master, Master, Master," he chants, wiggling beneath me, his body tense with need. "Please, please, please," he squirms.

"Not yet," I repeat as I pop off his cock, my gaze trailing up his shivering body. He's a mess; his frail chest flushed a pretty pink, nipples pointed and slightly darker than his porcelain skin. His eyes are squeezed tight, his face distorted in pleasure-pain, tears trailing down his cheeks, and into his damp hair. He's so beautiful, my Bunny, in the throes of passion.

"East!" he screams, when I dive back in between his thighs, sucking his full balls into my mouth. They're heavy on my tongue, reminding me of the place I've taken him to, of how I've unravelled him. "I can't," he sobs. "I can't, Master," he slurs. I release him from my mouth, the taste of him invading me.

"Too much?" I ask, suddenly concerned, reminding myself that he is new to this.

"Yes. No." He shakes his head.

"Bunny. Look at me," I beckon from between his thighs. "Look at me." His eyes flutter open, a deep umber, pupils blown wide. His mouth is slightly agape, his lips puffy. "You have to tell me if it's too much. I want to be a good master for you." He nods slowly, tears swimming in his eyes.

"You are," he whispers. "You are, East. You're so good. Only good." His gaze flickers before he looks away.

"But?" He continues to avoid my gaze, and I reach up, tweaking his left nipple to get his attention. Heat flashes through his eyes, precum oozing from his slit.

"It's so hard," he admits. "I've never..." He blushes even more. "Your mouth...it's...I can't." I can't help smiling. My shy, innocent Bunny. He needs me. Oh, how he needs me. I've never wanted to be needed before, I realise, always having found it a burden to have other people rely on me.

"Spread your thighs," I rasp. He looks at me wide-eyed but complies like the good Bunny he is. His cock rests across his abdomen and I grab it around the base, tightening my hand around his length as I start stroking him in firm, languid strokes. "Come for me, Bunny," I spur him on, knowing full well that once he has my permission, it's only a matter of seconds. "I want you to."

He comes on a deep sigh; creamy-white cum bursting from his cock, splashing across my knuckles and onto his stomach. His chest heaves, a deep moan leaving his throat, filling the room along with the scent of his release. He's everywhere, and I almost come from the sight of his blissful expression. *I did that*; my heart soars in my chest. *I did that to him like a good, caring master.* And with that realisation, something strange and wonderful happens. I feel... *content. Happy. Complete.* For the first time in my life, I feel complete. Fulfilled. His pleasure fulfils me. And it's everything all at once. It's nearly too much.

"Master?" his hesitant voice drifts towards me. I smile at him, my chest expanding from the sheer beauty of him. He's so perfect in the afterglow of his climax. So vibrant. I lean in over him as I move up his body, smearing his cum into his flawless skin. He squirms underneath me, his eyes glowing. "Master?" he repeats as I cover his entire body with mine, my face hovering above his, our lips so close that I can't feel where he ends and I begin. His breath becomes my breath, his heart beating against my chest, each beat echoing mine.

"You belong to me now, Bunny," I say, my voice nearly breaking on that last syllable.

"Yes." He nods, his eyes shining, his skin nearly translucent in the dim light.

"Only me," I croak, my eyes stinging, my chest burning.

"I only ever did," he says so easily, so obediently. "I've been waiting for you."

"Yes," I agree as something inside me, missing for so long, falls into place. "No one else will ever touch you or bring you pleasure, Benjamin," I add because, apparently, my possessiveness, when it comes to him, knows no bounds.

"No one else but you, East. I promise," he whispers as he reaches up and links his hands around my neck, tangling his fingers through my sweaty hair. Then something flashes in his eyes, a greediness that mirrors my possessiveness. "I belong to you now, just like you belong to me." I nod, my throat so tight from everything that he makes me feel and want and yearn for in this moment. I've never wanted to belong to anyone before, always seeing it as something suffocating and restricting. Only now, I can't imagine it being any other way. My life is meaningless unless I'm tied to him. "Say it," he breathes. "Say it, East."

"I belong to you, Benjamin. Only you. No one else." He beams at me, and then his stomach growls. Shit, I forgot about dinner; my body already so sated. "Don't move," I grin. "I got you soup. Chicken. I'll go reheat it now. Don't go anywhere," I add. He shakes his head, yawning, as he stretches out lazily on my bed.

"I love chicken soup," he slurs. Thank the fucking heavens.

"I got you dessert too." I puff out my chest because I'm on a fucking roll. I've got this *Master* thing down to a fucking T.

"You did?" he blinks at me. "What did you get?" he licks his lips.

"Carrot cake," I croak. "With cream cheese frosting."

"*Eeeeeekkkkk!!!!!*" he squeals, stomping his feet on the bed. "Just put a ring on it right now!" he grins, holding up his left hand, then pales, clasping both hands in front of his mouth. And I stare at him. I just stare, three words lodged in my throat. *Maybe I will, Bunny. Maybe I will.*

Chapter Twelve

F avourite things. The bright blue of my master's eyes. The deep frown between his dark blond brows when he studies me and thinks I don't notice. If I didn't know him by now, I would think I'd done something to upset or annoy him, but I know that it's just his '*East is serious and focused*' look. Because if I drop something on the floor—like I'll do in five seconds—he'll come rushing, fussing over me, making sure that I'm okay. See? The stack of empty boxes I was carrying has hardly hit the floor before he's at my side.

"Bunny," he grunts, raising a brow at me. "What have I told you? Leave the heavy stuff to me." I snort as he looks me up and down, wearing that frown I just want to lick at until it goes away. Because I love it the moment it reappears, my grumpy East returning to me. "Are you all right, darling?" he says, his voice growing softer, tender.

"Yes, East." I bat my eyelashes at him. "I'm quite all right." I suck on my bottom lip. He groans, shifting on his feet.

"Not now," he hisses, leaning in, his breath hot against my ear. "Not here."

"Yes, Master." I blink at him, going for my best *oblivious Bunny* look. He groans even louder.

"Don't." His piercing blue eyes sparkle and I know I'm in for it later. Maybe he'll finally stuff me with that plug. The one with the fluffy white bunny tail on it. I'm dying to get stuffed, to feel it's cool smoothness inside me, while my master hopefully fucks me with it while he blows me. I've asked him several times already, but he insists—*ugh*—that I'm not ready. What does he know? I'm so ready. Beyond ready.

Of course, East doesn't know that I've been practising at home. That's the thing about carrots; people don't realise they have so many purposes, aside from eating them, of course. They make perfect dildoes, actually. They're solid, hard, and you can get them in all sorts of shapes and sizes. There are slim ones and fat ones. Straight ones and crooked ones. They have ridges that feel amazing when you slide them in and out of your hole, just mind-blowingly amazing. I've been practising a lot. I want to be ready for my master for when he finally gives in. Which I hope is soon because, you know, this bunny is dying to be stuffed.

"Stop it," he grits, his pupils dilated, sweat beading across his oh so serious forehead. I want to lick that too. Just drink it right down.

"I didn't do anything," I pipe up.

"You were moaning," he says, his voice low, a subtle warning in the '*you*' that gets me instantly hard.

"Oh," I giggle. "Oopsie. Sorry about that." I blink. *Oblivious Bunny* is back. He shakes his head, but I don't miss the smile tugging at the right corner of his mouth that he's fruitlessly trying to fight. "Get back to work. There's a couple coming by at three to discuss some ideas for custom chocolate for their upcoming wedding."

"*Eeeep!*" I squeal, bouncing on my heels. "That's so exciting! I *love* weddings." I think. I've never been to one, but they strike me as the place where all pastel colours go to shine. Like one huge pastel colour convention. Like the Oscars only for pastel colours. And the Oscar goes to—

"You'll be on your best behaviour, won't you, Benjamin?" he interrupts my wayward thoughts, a glimmer in his eyes. "You'll be professional."

"Yes, East. Of course, I will." Shit, that was really short notice, but I guess I'll just have to come up with something. Spontaneous havoc. Because that's the thing about East's warnings. They're not *really* warnings. They're more like a game we play. A game we both love, that we can play over several hours while we work side by side in the shop until the air becomes so heady, so electric, that we have to close early and rush upstairs. Like when he just told me to be professional. That was a dare if I ever heard one. The next move is mine. We both know it. He's expecting it, but he has no idea what or when. That's the fun part.

He gives me a final glare, his mouth a straight line through his face, before he crouches and starts picking up the boxes.

"Go back to work." He's going for a bossy boss man now and it goes straight to my needy, carrot-deprived hole.

"Yes, Master." I shiver as I turn around, shuffling towards the back where I was restocking the shelves right before *the non-incident with the boxes*. I go back to working meticulously and efficiently, placing bags of cocoa powder on the shelves. As clumsy as I've been all my life, I'm not fidgety or antsy around East. Not anymore. His calm presence soothes me. His grumpiness settles me. He disappears into the back, probably to prepare for the wedding couple, and I go back to my *Favourite Things* list.

My master's golden hair when it falls into his eyes and the absentminded movement of his hand when he sweeps it back and it falls into place. His strong grip around my waist when he lifts me and places me on the counter like I weigh next to nothing, and kisses me silly right before the first customers arrive. His tongue in my ear, on my neck, along my chin. His warm, wet mouth on my cock, the fullness of his lips when they wrap around me, engulfing me with heat and the promise of endless pleasure. His hum; a deep, low vibration that sends desire shooting up my spine. His tongue, broad and rough against my sensitive cockhead. Those are all my favourite things. Things I never thought existed in my world. Things that were always beyond my grasp like a forbidden land. Things that are reserved only for the lucky few. Like East's smile when he sees me in the morning. The way his irises change colour. The teasing warmth in his voice when he calls me his *funny little thing*. I love it. I don't mind at all. Being a *thing*. As long as I get to be *his* thing.

The bell above the door chimes, followed by a lofty sing-songy, "Yoohoo! Easter, Darling!" and a wave of colours, prints, and flowy garments breezing by. It's like a unicorn floating on a rainbow wash through the shop, the heavy scent of gardenia invading the air all around me.

"Mum?" East appears from behind the counter, his hair deliciously disarrayed, and my fingers instantly tingle to brush through it. "What are you doing here?" He looks flustered, and a little annoyed, but mostly just filled by a subtle tenderness. I know all these small nuances about him by now. How the skin around his eyes and mouth softens when he's happy and himself.

"Oh shit, I forgot, didn't I?" Regret flashes across his face, his eyes oh so bright as he looks at the middle-aged woman who I assume is his mother, unless he calls all middle-aged women *Mum*.

Waving a gloved hand in front of her, she beams at him.

"Oh, never you mind, darling. Your father forgives you, assuming that, just like me, you've been busy." When she reaches him, she wraps him in what I can only assume is a proper mum hug because I've never had one. I've never felt my mother's arms around me, her body swallowing me right up, like East is swallowed up by a tangle of colourful garments right now. But that doesn't stop the feeling of longing coursing through my body; every cell wishing and yearning for something it's never had.

After a few seconds, East resurfaces, his eyes glassy as he smiles at his mother.

"I'm sorry I forgot," he murmurs.

"Never apologise for having a life," his mother shakes her head at him, golden-grey locks of hair imitating East's hair, surrounding her kind face. Then she tilts her head, her right gloved hand reaching for his chin, as she takes him in. "Something's different," she muses, turning his face from side to side. "You're...*happy?*" She sounds surprised, then suddenly turns around, her blue gaze moving around the shop until it zeroes in on the shelf I'm hiding behind. I was peeking over the top, but I quickly duck the moment I hear the *click-clack* of her heels across the hardwood floor, coming in my direction.

"Mum," East blurts, and I can tell that he's slightly worried. His steps are hurried as he follows her. "It's just—"

"Hello there!" Her bright face appears around the corner before she hurries towards me, her right hand stretched out in front of her. "I'm sorry I didn't see you when I came in, but I only had eyes for my dashing son," she smiles apologetically.

"I don't blame you," I blurt stupidly, my hand flying to my mouth when I realise my mistake. Mischief appears in her eyes as she tilts her head, throwing me a knowing look.

"Mum, this is Bun—Benjamin. My new shop assistant," my poor master rushes out, his eyes wild and worried, yet wonderfully warm.

"Benjamin!" she exclaims, grabbing a hold of my hand and shaking it furiously with the strength and intent of a Canadian lumberjack. "What a beautiful name. So nice to meet you, dearest. I'm East's mother, Dorothea Chrysanthemum Bennett. You probably haven't heard a thing about me because my son is funny like that, but here I am, alive and well." East's concerned eyes search mine, but my master needn't worry; I'm already spellbound and enamoured by his mother.

"Nice to meet you," I whisper, returning her smile. "Benjamin B. Sable," I add as I take her in. She's breath-taking, just like her son. A powerful presence that immediately makes you feel seen—truly seen—and included.

"*Sable*," she swoons, her gaze connecting with East's. "Oh, darling, now I see why you've been so preoccupied." Then she lowers her voice just a tad, a gentleness coating her next words. "He's lovely. Just lovely, darling." I suck in a breath, my legs nearly giving way beneath me, and I reach for the shelf to steady myself.

"Jesus, Mum," East sighs. "You can't go around saying stuff like that to strangers," he groans, rubbing at his chin.

"Why not?" she laughs. "He is. Lovely, that is. Don't you agree? Besides, Benjamin is not a stranger." She turns her focus back to me, a tenderness in her eyes that steals the air from my lungs. "I must apologise that I haven't got more time today, Benjamin, but I'm in a bit of a hurry. There's a sale at the flower shop, you see, and I don't want to miss it. Dutch tulips," she sighs. "Mr Glass promised to put some purple ones away for me. But you must come visit me. Soon." She clasps her hands in front of her chest. "Don't let my darling son keep you all to himself," she *tsks*, fondness swimming in her eyes. "Sunday before Easter, darling," she grabs East's chin in her right hand, shaking his head teasingly. "You'll come for lunch, and you'll bring young Benjamin." East groans, his shoulders tense, because if there's one thing my master hates, it's being told what to do. I can tell. "Say, '*Yes, Mum*,'" she smiles at him. "'*Whatever you say, Mum*.'"

"Yes, Mum," he agrees, sighing deeply. "Whatever you say, Mum. I'll be there." She raises a brow at her son, and he corrects himself. "*We'll* be there."

"Excellent!" She beams, then turns in a cloud of colours and gardenia, hurrying towards the door, disappearing just as quickly as she appeared, with a cheery *ta-ta* and a wave of her hand.

East visibly relaxes the moment the door closes behind her, the shop once again quiet.

"I like your mother," I blurt, moving towards him, accidentally taking an entire shelf of cocoa powder with me and sending the bags flying to the floor. "Oopsie." I wince.

"Everyone does," East groans, then laughs at me. "She knows, you know?" He reaches for me, shaking his head.

"What?" I breathe, going willingly, oh so willingly, burying my face against his neck when I reach him, sniffing him compulsively. I can't help it. I haven't sniffed him in hours. I need my dose of East.

"That you're special, Benjamin," he swallows. "Because you are."

"I am?" I say like the needy little bunny that I am.

"Of course you are." He breathes me in, his face disappearing into my hair. "Special to me." *Special to me.* Oh, what a joy to be special to someone as remarkable as my master. "Stay," he murmurs. "Stay tonight. Don't sneak out again. Please. I hate waking up to an empty bed." And against all reason, I find myself nodding. Because I *do* want to stay. So badly. And how can I say no to him when he's putting himself out there like this, all vulnerable and naked? "Yeah?" Relief courses through him as he squeezes me tighter against his chest. "You'll stay?"

"I'll stay," I say, praying to anything that might exist that it's not a mistake.

Chapter Thirteen

I don't think I've ever seen a couple as enamoured with each other as this American guy, Mason, and his British fiancé, Heaven. They've been here for at least 10 minutes, and Mason has not once removed his right hand from the small of his fiancé's back, a protectiveness emanating from him. While Heaven is *oohing* and *aahing* over the various chocolate creations that I've presented them with, tasting most of them, Mason has his gaze glued to him and him alone, his eyes swimming with pure adoration. I can't help but wonder if I look at Benjamin the same way. Can people tell that I'm completely and irrevocably under his spell, besotted like I've never been before? Lord, I hope not. That would be... *awful.* Then again... would it really be that awful if the world knew that it's happened? That lightning has struck. I mean, it only took my mother one glance at my face to see that I was happy. *Happy.* I'm happy.

Come to speak of it, why is Benjamin still in the back? I told him the wedding couple would be in this afternoon. He's been in the storage room for ages, supposedly just looking for some of the heart-shaped moulds to show to the couple from America. He's probably hiding. I've noticed he does that often when customers come into the shop. Unless it's one of the regulars like Mrs Glass and her grown daughter Penelope. Then he's ever so chatty and attentive, fussing all over Penelope, showing her his progress with the Easter window. And no, it's still not done, but that's mostly my fault because I can't keep my bloody hands to myself whenever he starts fondling that bloody bunny... especially when it's me, he should be fondling or whatever. Anyway, he adores Penelope. I don't know the specifics, only what Mrs Glass has told me. Penelope has an intellectual disability of some kind and will always be dependent on her parents. She lives at home where she helps Mr Glass in the nursery that he runs. But yeah, Benjamin is an absolute sweetheart with her.

"...in white?" Heaven looks at me expectantly.

"Sorry, what?" I reply a little too gruffly, interrupted during my umpteenth daydream today involving Benjamin. Heaven continues to smile at me, though. He must be around the same age as my Benjamin, while Mason appears to be slightly older than me. "Wouldn't you just love that too, Mase?" he bats his eyelashes at his fiancé, who seems to shake himself out of a love-induced stupor.

"Whatever you want, Evvie," he murmurs, cradling the much smaller guy against his chest. "Whatever you want, my love."

"Then I think I want them in white," Heaven says dreamily, already miles away at a white wedding banquet, nibbling on white chocolate leaves.

"Yes, absolutely!" Benjamin beams, popping out from the back like a Bunny-in-the-Box. So he was spying, was he now? I'm going to have to *talk* to him about that later. "We can absolutely make those for you with a coat of white chocolate. They'll look so pretty. We can even make different leaf shapes." I can tell by the tone of his voice that he's getting carried away, his enthusiasm for everything chocolate going straight to my cock.

"Oh, I would love that," Heaven smiles, looking up from the display of chocolates and over my shoulder, an odd expression slowly forming on his face, while Mason has gone slightly pale, tugging his fiancé protectively against his side.

"Oh, excuse me, this is my shop assistant, Benjam—" I say as I turn in Benjamin's direction and oh shit. Oh shitting hell. He's wearing the bunny ears. And the fluffy white wristbands. I know he does it when he's in the back or upstairs when we play our favourite game, 'Where has the naughty bunny gone?' but he always takes it off before entering the shop. He must've 'forgot.' Right.

"There's a man wearing bunny ears," Heaven states the obvious, and my ridiculous hope they hadn't noticed evaporates into thin air. Shit.

"Yes!" I blurt. "As you can see, we're *really* getting into the festive season here at *East of Eden!*" Benjamin nods eagerly, then adjusts his ears when they flop into his forehead. "More people ought to celebrate Easter," I continue, crap pouring out of my mouth with no end in sight, while Benjamin sniffs next to me. For fuck's sake, first Mum's surprise visit, now this. Will this day end already, so I can get my hands on Benjamin, carry him upstairs, and come my brains out on his perky arse?

"Oh, I love that!" Heaven near-squeals, blushing adorably, while Mason's gruff expression melts away like strawberry ice cream on a hot summer's day. As much as I pride myself on being the grumpiest grump to ever grump in His Majesty's Kingdom—or at the very least in Southern Kent—I have a feeling this Mason chap could out-grump me on any given day. After all, I'm just a small-town grump, whereas he's a big-city, executive-type grump.

"I'm a huge fan of Christmas myself," Heaven continues, stepping around the counter and right up in Benjamin's face. "Can I...can I touch them? They look soft," he sighs, nearly swooning on the spot, while Mason elicits something resembling a growl that spills over into a groan.

"Yes, of course!" Benjamin nods eagerly, smiling widely, as he throws me a quick glance, mouthing one of his infamous 'oopsies.' I just shrug because what can you do when you're dating a bunny? Wait, are we dating? Am I courting Benjamin? Huh, I'm going to have to revisit this later.

"Oh my God, Mase!" Heaven squeals, his face beaming brighter than a birthday cake. "You won't believe how soft these are!"

"I know, right?" Benjamin giggles, giving his head a little shake so the ears move side to side, looking adorable and delectable and all tempting things that start with the letter D; *drinkable, droolable, dickable.* Fuuuck. "East got them for me," he blinks. Sweet baby Jesus in a petting zoo, he did not just say that.

"Yes," I mumble, brushing a hand through my hair. "They're, uhm...they're part of our Easter uniform. You know, to get into the festive mood," I add, doing some weird gesture with my right arm to indicate that I am, in fact, in a festive mood. *Fuuuck.*

"East, I thought we didn't have—" Bunny insists on throwing me under the bus, which is definitely *not* part of his job description. *Neither is getting blown by your boss,* the voice of reason adds, just to mock me.

"I love them," Heaven near swoons, regarding Benjamin like he's just encountered his spirit animal or brother from another mother. "You're really pretty," he adds, blushing, and Mason growls again.

"Ahhh, thank you!" Benjamin giggles again. "So are you." For fuck's sake. "How come you're here? In England, I mean."

"We've been to Paris," Heaven sighs, and for a minute I'm afraid he's going to faint real Regency style. "To pick out my wedding outfit."

"Reeeaaally?" Benjamin's brown eyes grow impossibly big in his delicate face.

"Yeah," Heaven nods like he can't really believe it either. "And then we came here because I'm from England. We're going to a show tonight, and tomorrow we're visiting some of my old coworkers and friends."

"Oh, I see," Benjamin nods, looking a little disappointed they're not sticking around for longer.

"So, anyway," Mason starts, moving around the counter towards Heaven and Benjamin, and now I'm the one bloody growling because he's *waaay* too close to my pet now, mate. Fortunately, Mason doesn't seem to notice, but the small shiver running through Benjamin's body doesn't escape me. That little minx. He's playing with me. He's gonna get it later. "Evvie, sweetheart, we need to wrap this up. Like you said, we have a show tonight in London, remember?"

"Yes, Mase, I know," he nods, eyes still wide as saucers.

"Wow, you're tall," Benjamin gasps, tilting his head and taking Mason in. "He's even taller than you, East, and you're *tall*-tall." The hell he is. I've got at least a few inches on this Mason guy. "How did the two of you meet?" Benjamin continues, decorum flying out the window along with my impressive height, apparently.

"On a plane," Mason replies after a few seconds of silence, Heaven now transfixed by the wristbands. "We met on a plane," his voice softens, his shoulders relaxing.

"Oh, that's so romantic!" Benjamin hums. "You met on a plane and just flew right into love."

"Benjamin," I say, because this bunny is about to bounce right off to Bunnyland. But he doesn't seem to hear me, too engulfed in the romance of this couple.

"We can order some aeroplane moulds for you," he says. "We can make little chocolate planes for the wedding. With your initials on them."

"Oh em gee!" Heaven laughs. "That would be amazing. Wouldn't it be amazing, Mase?"

"Amazing," he drawls, looking slightly tired now, apparently just as over this bunny meet and greet as I was.

"Oh, I'm so excited," Benjamin bounces on his feet and Heaven laughs. "Me too."

"Sweetheart, we really have to get going." Mason takes one for the grumpy, growly boyfriend team—yeah, I've decided we're boyfriends. "You have our details, right?" he turns to me.

"Yes, absolutely." I accept the hand he's offering me, shaking it with relief, squeezing it just a little tighter than I normally would. *You're on my turf, Yankee. I'm the shit here in Chocolate Land.* I even get up on my toes, but yeah, Benjamin was right—they grow them tall in big old America.

"And it's really not a problem shipping it to Wyoming?" he adds.

"Of course not. We ship worldwide." I puff out my chest just a little. Because we do. People all over the world order from our webshop. Last week a bakery in Los Angeles ordered an entire case of T-shaped chocolates with orange cream filling. Yeah, no idea what that was about.

"Ugh, I wish we didn't have to go so soon." Heaven looks wistfully at the bunny ears.

"Me neither." Benjamin slumps, looking truly sad that his new bestie is about to bounce out of his life again. I guess I just have to work extra hard later on putting a smile back on his face. Maybe I'll finally plug him. He's been dying to get stuffed by that bunny tail, nagging me daily since I showed it to him. Yeah, I think I'm going to do that.

"C'mon Evvie." Mason grabs his fiancé's hand and tugs him out of the shop, the chime of the bell sounding sadder than ever.

"He was sooo pretty," Benjamin sighs once the door closes behind them. "Don't you think he was pretty, East? With that blond hair and those blue eyes."

"You're prettier," I grunt, surprising myself. "You're way prettier, Bunny."

Chapter Fourteen

I have no idea what's got into East, but the moment I turn the key in the door and close for the day, he's up in my face, a look in his eyes that's intense even for him. His chest is heaving like he's just run up and down the stairs five times, his hair dishevelled and deliciously wild.

"You," he breathes, his hot breath washing over my face. I blink, holding my breath.

"East?" I test the waters when he continues to stare me down. "Are you all right? You look a lit—"

"You," he says again, clenching his fists at his sides. "You drive me insane," he swallows. "Completely and utterly insane, Benjamin." He trembles, leaning in and catching my bottom lip between his teeth. I think I gasp into his mouth, my dick hardening instantly, my entire body alert. I decide then and there that I adore Crazy East. When he lets loose and discards his prim and proper exterior. When I manage to ruffle him up, and he gets all reckless. When he's... my East, wild and wondrous.

Hungrily, he sucks my lip into his mouth while his right hand finds a home around my throat, giving it a testing squeeze.

"You did that on purpose," he murmurs around my lip, before he releases it with a sloppy pop. I chase his mouth, shaking my head.

"I didn't, Master. I truly didn't. I forgot." My voice comes out in small, strained puffs as East's hand tightens around my throat. He tsks, tilting my head further backwards, my neck bent like a bowstring, bared for him, my big bad wolf. This bunny is ready to be devoured. My dick is so hard by now I'm leaking into my briefs, the warm stickiness pooling around my balls.

"What am I going to do with you, my bad little Bunny?"

"Oh, *shiiit*," I moan, swallowing behind his grip. Because I have a full list of things I want him to do to me and they mostly involve that bunny plug, his cock, or more preferably, both.

"Is that it?" he says, digging the tips of his fingers into my skin, while his other hand drops to my crotch, roughly grabbing my dick through my pants. "Is that what it'll take to make you finally behave like a good little bunny? You need to get fucked, Benjamin? Is that it? You need me to fuck that bad bunny right out of you?"

"Oh God," I pant, thrusting into his hand, my dick searching for friction, needing it so badly. "Oh God, yes, please, Master," I cry, fucking into his hand desperately. "I'll be good, then. I promise, Master. Then I'll be good."

"You will, won't you?" he murmurs, licking across my chin and up my cheek, his eyes searching mine for my innermost truth. I nod furiously as I try to capture his mouth with mine.

"I will. I promise, Master." I'm close to crying now, my entire body painfully tense, ready to explode. I think he must see it too—that I'm on edge and need him—because his eyes soften, warmth dancing amidst the cool blue as he nods. His mouth finds mine in a tender kiss, a kiss that's the secret East wants no one to know. East is gentle and kind behind his controlled exterior. He's wild and wonderful and mine. He may have said it, but I don't think he's fully realised it yet. I've known from the beginning, though—Easter Bennett is as much mine as I am his.

His tongue pushes its way into my mouth, demanding and hungry. I think I whimper, and before I know it, I'm flying, suspended in the air, then thrown effortlessly over his left shoulder. His right hand wraps firmly around the back of my left thigh and we start moving, my head bouncing as I focus on counting the furrows in the hardwood floor. I lose count somewhere between the counter and the stairs, and halfway up the staircase, I lose myself, completely and irrevocably. I'm so gone for him I'd gladly and gratefully put the rest of my life in his hands if he'd want it. He can do with it—and me—whatever he wants as long as I get to call him Master and he calls me Bunny. It's as simple and as complicated as that.

His heart beats against my abdomen, my hardness digging into his shoulder, my lust echoing his. As we reach the door to his flat, I think he'll put me down, but with skills that would put even Houdini to shame, he manages to open the door without letting go of me. The flat is dark, the evening wrapping around me like a familiar blanket, welcoming me. With determined strides, East moves straight for his bedroom, mumbling something under his breath.

"What?" I squeak.

"I said," he grunts, "I need to start exercising if I want a bunny for a boyfriend." *Boyfriend?* Boyfriend. A friend who's a boy is a boyfri—

"Stop it," he grits. "You heard me." Oh. So he *did* say that. My bunny ears didn't betray me. I feel like squealing but manage to hold it in by clenching my butt cheeks together and counting to three. If I were in a fantasy book right now, I'd be shooting baby bunnies out my butt at how excited I am.

As we enter the bedroom, he flips on the light, then carefully slides me down his body, putting me back on my now very unsteady, wobbly legs. His strong hands wrap around my upper arms, holding me in a firm grip, keeping me from sliding to the floor.

"I'm your boyfriend?" I whisper, testing the word on my tongue. It feels... *odd*, but somehow not wrong.

"Yes," he says, his eyes locked on mine. "Obviously." He shrugs.

"You mean it?" I croak. At the top of my list of things I was almost certain I'd never get to have was a boyfriend. Because who in their right mind would want me? *'Look at you, Benjamin! It's the third time this week! Honestly, I don't know what to do with you anymore. If I wasn't your mother...'*

"Most definitely." He nods, a softness in his voice that, until today, I thought was reserved only for me, but don't mind sharing it with his mum because I really like her. Then his gaze grows serious, and intense East back. "I would never lie to you, Benjamin. Never. Especially not about something like that." He laughs, his voice low and addictive. "If I haven't made myself clear by now, my intentions with you are genuine and...and constant." Oh shit, why does it always sound like my master has stepped right out of a Jane Austen novel? Who says *intentions* and *constant* these days? "I won't change my mind about you, about this," he says easily, like he's become a mind reader now too, aside from Houdini and an Austen protagonist.

I nod slowly, my gaze dipping to the floor, the tips of our shoes meeting. I zero in on his laces, which have suddenly become the most mesmerising thing in the world, apparently.

"Hey now," he says, tugging me against his chest, his right hand cradling the back of my head. "Why's that so hard to believe, darling?" *Darling.* Tears press behind my eyelids, my chest tightening.

"Because..." I sniff. "Because I'm not normal," I finally admit. "*Bunny* is not normal. I know he isn't. *I'm* not normal," I continue, anger building in my chest. I've lost count of the number of times that I've been told. '*Why can't you just act* normal, *Benjamin? I swear, sometimes I think you do it on purpose. Look at your brothers! How hard can it be to just act* normal *for five minutes?*'

"Benja—"

"I know he isn't," I cut him off, needing to get this off my chest. Needing him to understand me, *all* of me. "It's just...when I'm Bunny, I'm...free somehow. I know it sounds funny, but it's true. I only ever feel like myself, like truly myself, when I'm Bunny." *And who in their right mind would want a bunny as a boyfriend?*

"It makes sense," East says, his voice still soft and low.

"It does?" I sniff against his collarbone. "What does?"

"That I'd fall in love with someone like you, Benjamin," he says matter-of-factly. *Love. Love?* "Because fuck normal," he goes on like he hasn't just rocked this bunny's boat right off the love river. "Who really truly wants normal when they can have a bunny? When they can have *you.*" He pulls me away from his chest carefully, his eyes spilling over with want and tenderness and nothing but sincerity. "What is normal anyway, darling?" he hums. "Who's to say that what we have isn't as normal and as right as it comes?"

"You're in love with me?" I sniff, my stupid brain only just now catching up with him. He laughs, then tilts his head back, groaning.

"Yes! Of course, I am." He lifts his head again, his eyes boring into mine, his voice serious. "How could I not be, my darling Bunny? How could I not?"

"I'm...I'm in love with you too, East," I admit, because I think I have been from the moment he called me Bunny and perhaps even before that. "I love you too."

"Thank fuck," he smiles wider than ever before, his entire face lighting up, a pink blush creeping up his neck. He's so ridiculously sexy that I don't know what to do with myself. He's Robert Redford, covered in stardust, or a young Jeff Bridges, covered in the most tantalising dark chocolate. Yes, wouldn't that just have made *the Last Picture Show* even more epic if Jeff had been covered in chocolate? And because I'm me and because it's also true, I blurt the first thing that comes to mind, "I'm really horny."

"Jesus," he laughs again, shaking his head, blond locks all over the place.

"Will you..." I drop to my knees in front of him, my tongue heavy in my mouth, need building, threatening to tip me over the edge. "Will you please, please, *please* fuck this horny bunny tonight? With that plug, at least, but preferably also with your beautiful cock." I bat my eyelashes for good measure, then lean in and rub my cheek against his thigh, breathing him in. I even wiggle my nose like the good bunny I am. "Please, Master," I add, my words mingling with a soft purr, before they eventually drown in his groan.

Chapter Fifteen

"You've been practising," I say as I breach his hole carefully with the lube-slick plug. He gasps, his fists clenched around the sheets, as I slowly slide the cool object inside him. It's not thick; I was careful with that. As hard as it's been, I've been trying to go slowly with him. A deep moan leaves his mouth as he nods, his voice coming out in short puffs when he speaks, "Carrots." Fuck. Me. He widens his milky-white thighs, pushing them further back against his chest, his pink hole stretched beautifully around the silver plug.

"Carrots? Really?" Why am I not even surprised? Of course, my sweet Bunny would think of something like that.

"Please," he begs, his plump butt cheeks quivering with restraint, pearls of sweat beading along his forehead and temples. His eyes are closed, dark eyelashes resting against his flushed skin like tiny feathers. This bunny is running on instinct alone, and it's so fucking sexy, so I tell him that.

"You're so fucking sexy, baby." Oops, where the hell did that come from? I don't think he notices, though.

He's too far gone, consumed by his need for me. For *me*. I slide the plug all the way in, the fluffy tail covering his needy little hole, and he moans, whimpers, and shakes. *Fuuuck*. I take a step back, admiring him. He's completely naked, such a contrast to my fully dressed body, his skin flawless and flushed, as he squirms to adjust to the intrusive object. The bunny tail waggles a little from side to side as he moves his hips. It's going to be a pure fucking delight to fuck him finally. Give that hole a good and thorough fucking until it's moulded around the shape of my cock. Until it's—

"Master? Please," he cries out. "Please fuck me. I can't...I can't..." his eyes are wide open now, his teeth digging into his bottom lip.

"Ssshhh, darling," I coax. "I've got you. Your master's got you," I add, my chest filling with pride and gratitude that I get to call myself that. What a privilege. I carefully start sliding the plug out, a firm grip on the tail, before ever so slowly pushing it in again, twisting it on the way.

"Yes!" he gasps, moving beneath me, tilting his head back, his neck bared for me in the most delicious display of submission. "Yes," he sighs.

"You like that?" I rasp, leaning in over his body, as I find a slow rhythm to fuck him with. "You like having your tight hole fucked?"

"Uh-huh." He nods his head furiously, his brown curls spread across my pillow like a dark halo. "More," my greedy little beast begs, tilting his hips to meet the movement of my hand. So I give him more. I fuck him faster, harder, my other hand wrapped around both of his ankles to keep him somewhat still. His balls are tight, ready to burst, his dick pink and flushed, *slap-slap-slapping* against the back of his thighs. Although I have him completely bent to my will, his tiny body shaking with need, I have zero illusions that he's not as much the master of me as I am of him. It's a push and a pull; his need spurs me on, while my crumbling restraint fights to put a damper on him before we both crash all too soon.

My clothes are starting to feel suffocating, the need to have his naked skin against mine while I fuck him taking over. Without warning, I release the grip around his ankles, pull the plug from his arse and throw it on the bed before I start stripping at a furious pace, almost like I'm participating in the naked Olympics or some shit like that. Bunny screams, not from pain, but with annoyance, a disappointed "Hey!" shooting from his lips.

"Eager, are we?" I laugh as I bend to get rid of my socks. He throws me a frustrated look, his thighs resting against the sheets, still spread wide open for me. He looks pissy and even his hole seems to be pouting. "Don't worry, darling. You'll get the real deal soon enough." I smirk like I'm Burt Reynolds in some cheesy 70s movie. He huffs at me, but I still notice the small smile he's trying to swallow. Chucking my briefs, I grab my cock, giving it a few strokes just to take the edge off.

"Promises, promises," the little minx tsks, a challenge in his muddy-grey eyes that I feel like just fucking right out of him. But all in good time. Moving up the bed, I press kisses along his feet and ankles, while Benjamin giggles and wiggles. I lick along his calves, trying to give them both equal amounts of my attention before I nibble and bite my way up the back of his thighs. When I finally arrive where I'm supposed to be, resting between his welcoming thighs, our bodies flush against each other, my gaze searches his. I find his eyes worried, a hesitant frown between his brows. My chest tightens, worried that, after all, I've hurt him somehow or that he's changed his mind.

"What's wrong?" I ask, trying to hold back my concern. There's a wet sheen to his eyes now and I think I must have hurt him somehow.

"I hurt you." I wince, regret coursing through me.

"No!" he rushes out. "Never! Not you, East. Never you," he whispers. Oh, thank God.

"Then what is it? Please tell me, darling."

"I haven't done this before," he mumbles, his eyes two pools of watery greyish mud. Oh, my poor baby bunny. If that's it, then we're good. We're so good.

"I know." I smile, pressing a gentle kiss to the tip of his nose. "I'll be careful," I promise. "I'll go slow, darling."

"No!" He looks panicked. "If we go any slower, I'll die." He looks mortified and I can't help but laugh. "I mean it," he says. "I need you now, East." As if to stress the urgency, he pushes his hard dick against mine, all slick and pulsing.

"Then what is it?" I groan at the feel of him, *my love*, underneath and all around me. His scent, his taste, he's everywhere. Even if I aired out my bedroom for a lifetime, he would still be here. Always here. He's under my skin now, ingrained in every cell.

"I want to feel you. All of you, East. Nothing between us." His eyes are wide, expectant, a silent plea in them.

"Oh," I say as recognition dawns on me. "Are you sure?"

He nods eagerly, squeezing his thighs tighter around my hips.

"I'm sure," he says. "Completely."

"Okay." I nod. I was tested after my last failed relationship, and I don't fuck around. I'm on PrEP too, so I know I won't be putting him at risk, but still, the massiveness of what he's about to give me doesn't escape me. Warmth pools in my chest and now my bloody eyes are stinging. "I love you, Benjamin," I tell him what's in my heart. "I'll never hurt you, not intentionally."

"I know, Easter Bennett," he blurts. "I know you won't. There's only good in you. My East." Fuuuck.

"Now, I don't know about that." I chuckle, because I'm far from a saint, if that's what he thinks.

"I do!" He beams. "Now, please, will you finally fuck me, Master?" He bats his eyelashes endearingly.

"You sure?"

"Yes! For goodness' sake, East!" he glares at me.

"Very well. But if there's anything I do that you don't like, or that doesn't feel okay, you will tell me." I raise a brow at him, going for my best stern master look. He nods again, his hands finding my ass cheeks, his fingertips digging into my flesh.

"I will. I promise."

"Good Bunny. Because it may feel a little uncomfortable at first, but it's not supposed to hurt, all right?"

"Yes, Master," he says, all sugary sweet. Shit, I'm so fucked.

I move away from him slightly, my fingers finding his hole, testing it carefully. The plug has loosened him up a bit, but I'll need all my restraint. And lube. Lots of it. And perhaps a few revisits to my mother's god-awful attempt at carbonara, if I don't want to come the moment I slide inside him. Reaching for the lube beside my pillow, I slather my cock generously. Benjamin's eyes stay glued to my hand, a soft moan spilling from his lips. When I can't take it any longer—my hand a poor excuse for the real thing—I press his thighs all the way back against his chest again. His hole blinks at me, a light dusting of dark hair surrounding it.

"Hold on to your thighs, baby," I grit, and he complies immediately like the good little Bunny he is. Grabbing the base of my cock, I guide it towards his entrance, my fat, purple cockhead such a contrast against his pale skin. Although I'm not huge by any means, it still looks obscene and so fucking sexy, my cock hovering above his hole. Benjamin's dick is leaking, his balls drawn up tight, and I know it will be hard for him to control his release.

"This time," I say, "you can come whenever you want." I'm met by a relieved nod of his head and a muffled whimper. "You ready?"

"Yes, Master," he says, his voice the perfect mix of eager and submissive. I smear the excess lube from my fingers across his hole and he startles like I've shocked him. He's so sensitive, and it's all me, I tell myself. He wants *me*. Easter. His master.

Ever so carefully, I breach him, gritting my teeth to the point of pain. I'm met with restriction at first as he tenses around me.

"Breathe, baby," I coax, giving him time to get used to the pressure around his entrance. He nods, his face the image of concentration. "You okay?"

"Yes," he murmurs, shaking a bit. "Yes. Go on."

"Relax for me, darling. I've got you," I say as I push against the tight ring of muscle, feeling it relaxing slightly around me. He's warm and soft and *oh so right* as he, by some miracle, welcomes me inside him, a succession of sweet whimpers falling from his lips.

"Oooh," he gasps. "Oh, that's..." His voice tips into a deep moan as I pull out a little, only to slide further in. "Oh, my word," he moans again, and the softness of his voice, combined with the wet heat of him, sends flames licking down my spine. *Mine*, the wolf in me growls as I push all the way in, my groin flush against his butt, my cock splitting him wide open for me.

"Ahhhh," he hisses, squirming underneath me, his fingers tearing at my skin. "East, East, East," he chants. "That's so..." he whimpers. "That's just so..."

"I know, darling," I say, my voice heavy with emotion and desire. "I know." I give him as much time as I can to adjust to my size without combusting completely. When he relaxes beneath me, his hole pulsing around me, I know he's ready. I start fucking him in a slow, steady rhythm until I eventually lose myself in him. I lose track of time, and as I forget myself, the only thing that matters becomes him. How he moans, how he moves, how he makes me feel. Because, boy, does he make me feel everything all at once. The sound of our skin slapping against each other fills the room, along with the heady scent of our combined lust. His sweetness. God, his sweetness. It does something to me that's beyond my control.

"Fuck, you feel so good," I admit. "So, so good." He hums around me, meeting my thrusts eagerly, fucking me as much as I am him at this point. "You like riding my cock, baby? You like my big, fat cock tearing you wide open?"

"Uh-huh," he pants, his chest heaving. "I love it, Master. I love your big, fat cock so much."

"You do, don't you? You *need* it, right Benjamin?"

"I do," he smiles, his eyes wild, delirious. "I do. Never stop. Never, ever stop, East. Fuck me like there's no tomorrow." Oh shit. His words are like gasoline on the fire burning inside me. I fuck him harder, deeper, faster, his tiny body a rag doll beneath me, taking my thrusts, my cock, like the best little bunny in the world. I'm close, but I don't want this feeling to end. I want it to last until I burn. Until we burn together.

"You're mine, Benjamin." I fuck the imprint of my cock into him permanently. "You know that, right, baby?" And if I ever had any illusions that I wasn't a corny man at the core, they're blown to smithereens right this minute.

"There's no buyer's remorse on this cock. Once you take it, it's yours."

Then I feel it, how he clenches around me, his inner walls squeezing me tighter, until a scream tears from his lips.

"*Ahhhh*. East? East?" His hands drop from my ass, sliding up my back, grabbing desperately at my shoulders, while he comes.

"I'm here, my beautiful, beautiful darling. I'm right here," I croak as I feel the warmth of his cum as it hits my stomach. The scent of him intensifies, his sweet cum going straight to my balls, triggering my own climax. My cock swells inside him, and then there's nothing else but white-hot pleasure as I come inside him, my release filling him.

"I love you," he whispers, his voice vibrating with the aftermath of his orgasm. "I love you so much, Master."

"I love you too," I pant. "So, so much, my sweet darling."

"Thank you," he sighs, and I can't help laughing, the sound bursting from my chest uninhibited. He winces, my cock still inside him.

"I'm the one who should be thanking you." I laugh again as I continue to fuck him, to fuck my cum as deep inside of him as I can. Until I can taste myself on his tongue when I kiss him goodnight. "For this precious gift you've just given me."

"It's nothing," he drawls. "Nothing compared to what you've given me." Then he yawns, all sated and soft, and the next second, he's gone, passed out on my cock, a content smile on his lips. Shit, I fucked my Bunny into a coma. He looks so peaceful, his dark lashes moist—from tears, perhaps. Or sweat. I can't tell. His cheeks are scarlet and burning, and the soft swell of his chin makes him look much younger than his years. His warm breath comes out in small puffs, the occasional snore bubbling from his lips. God, I love him. He's mine now, truly mine. I'm never giving him up. He has my cum inside him. No one has ever had my cum inside them. That's special, right? It has to be.

As I slip from his hole, he murmurs something unintelligible but doesn't wake. I tiptoe to the bathroom and find a washcloth that I hold under the warm water. He's still asleep as I sit down next to him and carefully swipe the warm cloth along his crease and around his hole. Then I clean myself, wiping his cum from my stomach, promising myself that next time he comes, it'll be down my throat. Discarding the cloth on the floor, I lie down next to him, pulling the duvet up around us, all the way to his chin, tucking him in. I manoeuvre him so his head rests against my chest, my arms wrapped solidly around him. He stirs but doesn't wake, snuggling against my chest hair. I fall asleep in minutes with his name—the name I've given him—on my lips. *Bunny. My Bunny.*

Sometime later, when it's still dark, he jolts awake and sits up, startled, his hair all wild as he rubs his eyes.

"Benjamin?" I say, sleep gone from my body within seconds, completely tuned into him. "Are you okay? Are you in pain? Do you need me to get you something?" I bombard him with questions. He turns and looks at me, his expression unreadable.

"East?"

"Yes, darling."

"If it becomes too much, then tell me. I know I can be too much at times." His eyes are huge and filled with concern.

"Hey, where's this coming from?" He blinks at me, his bottom lip quivering. "Benjamin, you don't ever have to hide your true self from me. Not ever."

"You say that now, but..."

"I mean it. Never hide from me. You're beautiful when you're Bunny *and* when you're Benjamin. Darling, you just gave me the most precious gift of my life. You make me so happy. Happier than I ever thought possible."

"Are you sure?" he whispers.

"Absolutely. Never been more sure about anything in my life," I admit, recognising the truth of my words. I never thought life could have this much joy in store for a grumpy arsehole like me.

"I want to believe that so much. I really do. I want to believe *you* so much." He looks truly torn.

"Then believe it."

"It's hard when you've been told your entire life that you're wrong." He slumps his shoulders, and I reach out and tug him against my chest.

"There's nothing wrong with you, Benjamin," I speak against the crown of his head. "Not a single thing. They, whoever made you believe that, whoever made you feel wrong...they're the ones who are wrong. Not you, my darling. Not you. Never you. You're perfect."

He tilts his head, looking up at me. "You really mean it, don't you, East?"

"I do." I smile. "Now, let's sleep, baby. Let's sleep."

Chapter Sixteen

As soon as I wake, I know that I've slept in for the first time in, perhaps, ever. The bright spring sun bursts through the thin linen curtains, adding a warm glow to the room. I can feel it on my face and I chuckle to myself. Even as a child, I would never sleep in, always the first one in the house to rise, leading my own secret life watching *Blue Peter* and eating *Ricicles* from the box before the rest of the house woke. I guess that's what love does to you. Makes you sated and lazy. Fuck. I'm in love. In love. With Benjamin. With the sweetest, sexiest soul to ever walk this earth. It feels... *strange.* To have handed my heart over to someone, but still, it also feels like it couldn't be any other way. That it was always going to end up like this—he and I, in love—from the moment he walked into my shop for the first time. *Soulmates.* I used to laugh at people when they spoke of *the one and only.* The one that was made *just for them.* Now I *am* them. I'm a believer. Benjamin, with his massive heart and vibrant personality, has turned me into a believer.

A sudden feeling of loss invades my chest, and I instinctively turn and reach for him, only to find his side of the bed cold and empty. Fuck, he did leave, after all. Even when he promised he would stay. My elusive little Bunny. I'm going to have to talk to him about that later, but right now, I'm just too goddamn lazy, and I need a dose of bunny. I reach for his pillow, burying my face in it, breathing in the remnants of his sweet, intoxicating scent. The moment I breathe him in, my cock awakens, hungry for him, and I groan pathetically into the fabric. Last night was everything. Being inside him. The sweet whimpers and moans that I pulled from his body. The way he made me feel. I'd never been able to let go like that before, but being inside his warm, tight hole, moving with him, was so liberating I could finally just let go.

I inhale again, rubbing my nose across the pillow, pretending it's him. Then, little by little, a tangy smell hits me. It's not sharp, but it tickles my nose. It takes a few seconds for my brain to recognise the smell and match it with a word, but when it does, my heart sinks. *Urine.* The smell is, without a doubt, the smell of urine.

I sit up, confused, taking in Benjamin's side of the bed, and at first, I don't notice it. But as my eyes get used to the white sheets, I see it. In the middle of the indent that his body has left behind, there's a fairly large spot, slightly darker than the rest, with a yellowish tint to it. I swallow, reaching out my hand and brushing my fingers along the still-damp material. It's cold and my heart sinks again because it means that he must have left when it was still dark outside. My poor Bunny, sneaking away like a thief in the night. My heart breaks for him. For how he must've felt waking up, wet and cold and... oh Christ, the shame. The shame. My eyes sting, a mix of sadness and anger building inside me.

Sadness because he felt he had to leave. Anger because he felt he had to leave. Did he think that I... that I would be mad? Upset? Repulsed? Perhaps he did, but Jesus, nothing that beautiful man does will ever repulse me. Nothing.

Within seconds, the anger fades, and all that's left is only a feeling of all-consuming worry. I have to find him, hold him, reassure him that everything is okay. To tell him nothing has changed between now and last night when I told him I love him. Because I do. I love him with a fierceness that should scare me, but which only makes me feel more complete than I ever have before. If Benjamin thinks that wetting the bed is a deal-breaker, he's got another thing coming. No fucking way. It's not even close to being a deal-breaker. Although, to him, my lovely, wonderful darling, it probably feels like the end of the world right now.

My stomach does a weird somersault, and a pitiful yelp leaves my mouth. My body aches for him, protesting his absence, and I know what I need to do. I have to find him and bring him back home. But first I have an errand to make. Because I need to *show* him he's claimed a place in my life that is irrevocably his. That was always his. And a little pee is not going to come between us. Although I don't understand why it happened or if it's happened before, I'm determined that we will overcome it. I just need to show him we can. When I claimed him as mine, I meant all of him; I realise that now. Every single part of him. Just like he accepts every part of me, from my grumpiness to my bossy nature. For my need to dominate. All of it.

Within seconds, I'm out of bed, pulling on the discarded clothes I wore the day before. I sniff the shirt and deem it acceptable. I'm in a hurry. I'm a man with a plan and I can't be bothered with meaningless things like a wrinkled cotton shirt or... or no briefs. Every second away from Benjamin becomes my sworn enemy. A mountain I must climb. A giant sea monster I must defeat. Because I know he will use every single second we're apart convincing himself that it's over. That *we* are over. When we're not. We're not near being over. I'm not done with my bunny. I'll never be fucking done with him.

As I chase down the stairs, nearly stumbling on the second last step, centimetres away from bashing my head against the wall, I'm rewriting the wedding vows in my head. *Will you take this Bunny. For better or for worse. Pee or no pee. In sickness and in health.* I will. I do. I so do. Urine be damned.

In my office, I tear through the drawers, pulling papers from them and throwing them left and right until I find what I'm looking for.

"Aha!" I exclaim to no one at all, holding Benjamin's CV victoriously above my head, like the head of a dragon I've just slain. As I skim through his neat handwriting, my stomach does another one of those weird somersaults, where it feels like it's trying to turn me inside out. God, I miss him. I hold the paper to my nose and breathe it in, but there's no trace of him, my Bunny, just the dull, bland smell of paper. *Fuuuck.* Is this what withdrawal feels like? I guess it is.

I sigh with relief when I notice an address written at the very bottom, just below his name. It's not far from here, the street. Checking my watch, I jog to the door, swiping my coat from the hanger on the way. If I hurry to the shop, I can be back here by noon, get the bedroom sorted, and be at Benjamin's place shortly after. It won't take me long to put my *get-my-bunny-back* plan into action. I can have him back in my arms where he belongs before I know it. My chest and arms ache with the phantom feel of him and I hug myself, closing my eyes, pretending it's him, my love. Then I suck in a breath, shaking my shoulders and bouncing on my feet—almost like I'm getting ready to take down Rocky himself—before I throw the door open and stalk down the street like a madman.

Chapter Seventeen

I knew I shouldn't have stayed. I only have myself to blame. I tried to stay awake long after East had fallen asleep, but it was just too hard; my body spent and sated after he'd fucked me. Then, when I woke, I instantly realised my mistake, the sheets cold and clammy beneath me, my wet briefs sticking to my skin as a cruel reminder that I don't deserve this. That I don't deserve him. I've been crying non-stop, and it must be afternoon by now because the light outside Mr Harvey's living room window is starting to fade. He found me this morning, a shivering sobbing mess between the neat rows of radishes and spring onion I sowed the weekend before.

'*Come now, Laddy,*' his familiar, comforting voice washed over me as he carefully pulled me to my feet. '*You're getting cold here. Come. Come with me, son.*' I don't recall how we got here, to Mr Harvey's house, or what happened afterwards, but I think I must've had some tea because there's a bitter taste on my tongue. Or maybe it's just the shame I can taste. There's only shame now in my world. And the throbbing pain in my chest over losing him, my master. Shame and loss. The shame is familiar; it was, after all, my silent companion growing up, always feeling misplaced in my family. Like a ghost, almost. The loss I only felt once before, when they took Bunny away from me, and although it was all-consuming and devastating, it was nothing compared to how I'm feeling right now. Because with East I felt seen. *He* made me feel seen and wanted. And not just that, no, it was like he was changing too. Because of me. *I* made him happy. *I* made him smile. I even made him laugh with abandon at times. And now it's all ruined. I guess my parents were right. I *do* ruin everything.

I sniff as treacherous tears try to break free from my eyes. I don't want to cry again. Not like this morning when it was still dark, and I broke to pieces in Mr Harvey's garden. I focus on the repetitive tick-tock of Mr Harvey's old clock. *Tick-tock. Tick-tock.* After a while, as I linger in a state between awake and asleep, the monotonous sound blends in with something else. There's a familiarity to it I can't quite place until my mind zeroes in on a soft murmur coming from the kitchen. Oh. It's probably Mr Harvey's favourite radio programme, *Memory Lane Radio.* He listens to it for hours, humming along to Sinatra and Aretha. I once caught him singing into a spoon, swaying his hips from side to side, crooning along to 'New York, New York.'

There's no music though. Only voices. Mr Harvey's deep raspy voice and then a smooth, velvety one I know better than I know the beat of my own heart. Although low, there's a stubborn insistence to it, with a pleading undertone. *East.* It sounds like him, only it can't be, can it? And yet, there's no mistake. It's him. Oh, crappy carrot cake, he's come to fire me. To let me go. I know it. I just know it. My heart sinks and then breaks, before finally crumbling to the living room carpet.

Mr Harvey's voice increases in volume, soft steps coming down the hallway, followed by louder, more eager ones. Oh no. I can't. I just can't. Not yet. I'm not ready. Who am I kidding? I'll never be ready. Now that I know what real love feels like, I can't go back to that cold, dull existence that used to be my life. It's like tasting the darkest, richest chocolate and then being told that you can never have it again. Anger grows inside me. It's not bloody fair! It's not. *They* did this to me; my *'family.'* They turned me into this frightened creature. I hate them. I hate them so mu—

"Let me go in first," Mr Harvey says behind the slightly ajar door. "He might still be asleep, the lad. We don't want to spook him."

"Right, right," East agrees, but the strain in his voice doesn't elude me. Impatience. He's impatient to get this over with.

The door creaks open, and Mr Harvey's worried face appears behind it. He seems to hesitate, but when he notices that I'm awake, he enters.

"Son, there's someone here to see you." I swallow and the tears threaten to fall again. *Someone.* The man I love more than anything. My heart. Mr Harvey tilts his head, taking me in. I must look a right fright. "But if you're not up to it, I'll tell him to come back."

I shake my head, swallowing back the bile starting to rise in my throat. I clench my fists in the woollen duvet that smells of Mr Harvey and everything that's good and right in this world. Breathing through my nose, I focus on Mr Harvey's kind face. He still loves me. At the end of the day, Mr Harvey still loves me. That has to be enough. When I feel like I'm not going to puke, scream, or pass out, I nod.

"It's okay, Mr Harvey. You can let him in. I'm okay." I'm not. I'll never be okay again. I'm the most un-okayistest person in the world.

"You sure, lad?" Mr Harvey shifts on his feet, a protectiveness emanating off him that is at least a little comforting. I wonder if East has told him what I've done? No, he wouldn't. I'm sure of that at least.

"Yes. Thank you." I offer him a weak smile, brushing my fingers through my unruly hair, smoothing the wayward locks somewhat.

"All right then. But you call if you need me, won't you? I'll be right down in the kitchen, so you just give me a shout."

"I will," I whisper, sniffing the tears away. *I love you, Mr Harvey*, I want to tell him. *I love you so much.* He's the father I always wanted, a good, kind man. The father I should have had in a perfect world. But the world isn't perfect.

He nods again, then disappears behind the door, and I get just a few seconds to prepare myself before he appears. My East. No, not *my* East. He's not my East. Not anymore.

"Benjamin!" he rushes out, his hands held out in front of him like I'm a wild animal that he's afraid of spooking. "Darling," he croaks, rushing to my side, his eyes spilling over with worry. It takes my mind a few seconds to wrap itself around the desperate *darling*, and a few more to notice that he's shaking like a baby leaf on a cruel April day.

"I was so worried," he blurts, kneeling on the carpet next to the sofa, carefully reaching for my hands. "So worried," he repeats, his fingers tangling through mine, his blue eyes dark with concern. My initial thought is that he hasn't noticed yet. That he hasn't noticed how I've soiled his bed, ruined the very place where we made love for the first—and only—time. My mind goes to all sorts of places; I could run back to the flat and hide the evidence of my shame before he notices or I could run away and join a circus that hires bunnies or I could—"I'm so sorry, Benjamin," he says, his eyes brimming with... *tears.* Yes, there's no mistake. The blue is swimming in watery pools of more blue, that deep frown digging into his skin between his golden brows. "I'm so sorry, my darling," he says, squeezing my fingers between his, his voice growing in insistence. "I didn't know." He gets up from the floor and carefully sits down next to me on the sofa. Releasing my hands, he cradles my cheeks gently, before he leans in and presses a tender kiss to my forehead. "I didn't know, my sweet, sweet Bunny."

And I break. I break into a thousand tiny pieces. *Bunny.* I'm still Bunny. It's not pretty, my breakdown. It's not like in the movies where silent, sophisticated tears trail down the hero's cheeks, while he sobs quietly and composed. It's not stoic and controlled. It's not. It's ugly-crying times one hundred. There's snot and snorts and gulps. There are hiccups, and I even think I throw up in my mouth a little once the stress and anguish have left my body.

"East," I squeak, tugging at his shirt. I blink, taking him in, and he looks a right mess, just like me. He looks worn and ruffled. He's even wearing the same shirt as yesterday. He looks wrecked, but he doesn't look angry, nor repulsed. He doesn't.

"Come here," he rasps, pulling me against his chest, swallowing me right up, his familiar scent with an edge of sweat engulfing me, calming my heart. He murmurs something against my left ear while he presses tender kisses against my neck. *Nothing.* It sounds like *nothing.*

"East," I whimper, his kisses doing things to me that are not appropriate for Mr Harvey's living room. "I...I didn't mean to do it." He freezes, his lips lingering against my neck. "I did it a lot as a child, but not so much anymore. Only when…only when I get excited." My cheeks burn with shame, and my throat is itchy from the words leaving my mouth. "Or when I forget myself," I admit. "I guess I must've forgotten myself last night." There. That's it. Now he knows. He knows that I've done it before and that it can happen again.

"I forget myself when I'm with you, too," he says. And I feel the smile against my skin just before he releases himself and his face is right in front of my face. "I forget about everything when I'm with you, Benjamin, and it's just the best fucking feeling in the world." His blue eyes are bright, beaming, with nothing but sincerity reflected in the intense cerulean. "Time stops. My mind quiets down. And there's only you." He leans in, his lips finding mine in a featherlight kiss, his warm tongue dancing along my bottom lip, nibbling at it, sucking it into his mouth. "Nothing," he murmurs again, and I giggle.

"What?"

"What *what*?" he smiles against my lips, humming contentedly like a little bee on the first day of spring.

"What '*nothing*?'" I smile back, my lips buzzing.

"Oh," he laughs. "I keep getting distracted from what I want to say. What I wanted to tell you." He lets go of my mouth and gazes at me. He looks drunk, my East. "You're so bloody distracting," he drawls. "So bloody distracting."

"Sorry." I giggle again. "What did you want to tell me?" His expression turns serious then, the frown back between his brows, and my fingers itch to rub it away. His hands find my shoulders, wrapping around them, holding me in a fierce grip.

"Nothing," he starts. "Nothing will *ever* change my mind about you, Benjamin. About us. Nothing in this world can ever change the fact that I am hopelessly and irrevocably in love with you." A weird sound leaves my lips because he can't possibly mean that. I must still be asleep. This is some desperate dream my mind has conjured because reality is just too hard to deal with. This is a denial dream. It has to be.

"Are we awake?" I blurt, blinking my eyes rapidly to see if he disappears. He snorts, his warm breath hitting my chin.

"Darling, are you listening to me?" he says more firmly, shaking my shoulders gently. I nod slowly.

"Yes, East. I'm listening. But..."

"But what?"

"But I'm afraid that I'm dreaming. That you're not real," I whisper. He sighs deeply, his grip on my shoulders growing tighter.

"You're not dreaming, Benjamin. This is real. We are real, you and me. We are as real as they come." He pauses as he seems to consider something, then nods. "Can I tell you a secret?" he says, a vulnerability to his voice that I've never heard before.

"Yes. Anything," I whisper.

"I only like myself when I'm with you, Benjamin. You make me the kind of person I want to be. Carefree and less uptight. A little reckless even. I wasn't always a grumpy arsehole. A cynic. I was a happy child. I used to look forward to silly things like Easter or my birthday or the first day of spring. I just...I can't pinpoint how or exactly when it happened. It just sort of did. The only thing I cared about aside from my mother was chocolate. Because I could mould it the way I wanted it to be. I could make these perfect pieces of chocolate that people would praise. The chocolate didn't want anything back in return. It didn't ask anything of me. It didn't..." he shakes his head wistfully.

"What?" I breathe because, wow, East has never been this open and honest with me before.

"It didn't challenge me," he says. "Not like you do."

"I challenge you?" I ask, stunned out of my mind.

"You do," he smiles.

"How? How do I challenge you?" He squirms, then groans slightly, releasing his grip on my shoulders and tugging at his hair instead.

"You make me remember what it's like to have *fun*." He says the word fun like one would say *turd* or *puke*, while he wrinkles his nose. I can't help snorting and he throws me a glare. "Don't play with me, Bunny," he says, an unspoken challenge in his voice. "Fun is dangerous for grumps like me, don't you know?" I shake my head. I don't. "It makes us believe life can be *fun* and that we can have it, a happy life with laughter and joy and..."

"And?" I hold my breath.

"And love," he says, looking crestfallen.

"And you don't want that?" I reach out and brush my hand along his scruffy chin, the familiar scratchiness making my thighs shiver.

"I do," he says, leaning into my touch. "I do want it. I want it so badly, Benjamin. With you."

"But?" My hand slides to the back of his neck, sweeping through his smooth gilded strands that are like liquid gold. He's golden, my East.

"I'm afraid," he admits. "I'm afraid that..." He catches himself, then deflates. "When my dad died, it's like my mum ceased to exist. At least, it felt like that for a long time. There was nothing...I couldn't do anything. It was almost as if I'd lost her, too. She didn't say it, but it wasn't hard for me to see it." His chin dips and I reach for him, circling my arms around his neck.

"See what?" I ask when he stays silent, carding my fingers through his silken strands. He licks his lips.

"That she wanted to go where he was. That she was done with this world." He winces. "Done with *me*." He looks like a boy now, or at least a reflection of the boy who lost everything all at once.

"How old were you?" I swallow.

"Twelve. I was twelve."

"Oh, East."

"It's okay," he shakes himself. "She came back eventually." He smiles half-heartedly.

"But the fear that you could lose her again stayed," I finish for him. He nods, looking straight at me.

"When I woke up this morning, and you were gone..." A tear breaks free from his lashes and starts the lonely journey down his stubbled cheek. "It was like my heart stopped. Like truly, literally stopped. Like it no longer had any purpose." I nod, because I know what he means. I've felt the same way all day; every second, minute, hour spent away from him pure torture.

"You're my purpose, Benjamin. You are *my* Bunny. My heart. And it's scary as hell, but I can't—I *don't*—want to be without it. Without *you*." More tears break free from his eyes, and he looks so young and vulnerable and just altogether lovely.

"I don't want to be without you either," I croak. "You're my purpose, too. I was meant to be your Bunny, just like you were meant to be my Master."

"Does that mean you're coming home?" He lights up, gold now morphing into diamonds before my very eyes. He's glowing, my beautiful, beautiful master. He's glowing with the same hope that's taking over my heart. A raw, needy kind of hope.

"If you want me to." I nod.

"I do. I want you to," he rushes out.

"But it might happen again," I whisper.

"I know," he says solemnly. "I know, but it doesn't matter. We'll figure it out. Pee or no pee, you're it for me, Benjamin."

"Pee or no pee?" I snort, a thousand giggles dancing in my chest.

"Yeah, yeah, whatever. It sounded better in my head," he grunts. "It sounded *romantic*." Again, he pronounces the word like one would say *haemorrhoid* or *infected toenail*.

"Romantic?" I tease. "Yes, God forbid, East. That would be dreadful." I laugh.

"Don't play with me, Bunny," he non-warns me again, raising a brow at me.

"Or what?" I blink innocently, and he just groans, and growls, and scowls like the wonderful man he is, Master. My man.

"You'll see," he smirks and my heart sings 'Yes, *yes. Show me. Show me everything.*'

Chapter Eighteen

P art of me is freaking out as I lead him through the
flat towards my bedroom, but mostly I'm just excited, almost giddy. It feels like a weight has been lifted
from my shoulders, sharing my father's death and my
mother's retreat from the world with him. I hope—no,
I pray—my surprise for him will be the ultimate proof I
meant what I said. That nothing, absolutely nothing, can
change how I feel about him, my Bunny. His right hand is
securely clasped in mine while the other is fisted tightly
in my shirt collar like he's afraid I'll somehow dissolve
into thin air. He's tucked against my side and although
it's slightly awkward walking like this, I think we both
need it. The closeness. The quiet comfort of the physical
connection. The reassurance that we are unbreakable.

Fuck, I almost wasn't allowed to take Benjamin with
me. Once I'd persuaded him to come back, Mr Harvey
pulled out a kitchen chair and said '*Sit, young man!*'
real Scotland Yard style. I heard Benjamin snort behind
me and I'm not sure if it was because someone was
out-bossing his boss or because Mr Harvey referred to
me as young. Never mind. I'd rather have my Bunny

snorting than crying any day of the week. I won't go into details, but let's just say that dear old Henry VIII would have loved for Mr Harvey to have been one of his royal interrogators. Once he was satisfied that my intentions were sincere, he pulled Benjamin into a bear hug and murmured something against his ear that made Benjamin sniffle like I'd never heard him sniffle before.

"East?" Benjamin tugs at my shirt impatiently, frowning at me. "How much longer are we gonna stare at your door?" He smiles at me knowingly, then bats his dark brown eyelashes.

"Right," I grunt, reaching around him and opening the door. As soon as I open it, I smell the intense fragrance of the tulips, and I know he does, too, because he wrinkles his nose adorably and peeks inside. "Go on," I laugh and give him a gentle push. He stumbles, but I catch him around his waist and he giggles against my chest. And that's how we enter the room, me turning him around, half-pushing him inside with my arms wrapped around him from behind. A deep sigh leaves his chest when his gaze connects with the generous vase of lavender tulips on the nightstand next to his side of the bed. *His side.*

"Are those for me?" he asks, his voice breathy, as he leans back against my chest and looks up at me. I nod and if I could take a forever photo of Benjamin to store away in my mind, this would be it. The way he's looking at me right now. Like I just hung the bloody moon. My chest fills with pride and love, as I nod and rasp, "Yes, darling. Those are for you."

"I love them," he whispers. "Lavender is my favourite colour."

"I know," I say, because although he's never told me, I somehow know. Just like I know that the sun rises in the East and sets in the West, I know everything important about him, my Bunny. His smile takes over his entire face, lighting up his muddy-grey eyes until they're sparkling like two large pieces of moonstone. "They smell wonderful," he whispers. "Thank you, East." I just nod at him, my heart in my throat, because I know what he means. They smell of spring and hope and new beginnings.

"You're welcome, darling," I hum against his lips. I kiss him tenderly, sucking his plump bottom lip into my mouth, feeling him squirm with need and then melt against me pliantly. I force my tongue into his mouth, and he meets me willingly, his fingers digging into my pecs, like he wants to crawl all the way inside me and live there, right next to my heart.

"East," he moans as he starts humping my left thigh, grinding his hard dick against my pants. "I'm gonna come if you keep this up."

"Don't." I bite into his lip, and he whimpers. "Don't come yet. There's more."

"More?" He frowns, panting. "But East..." He shakes his head as he blinks at me, all love-drunk and adoring. "The tulips..." He gestures at the nightstand.

"There's more," I say simply, untangling his fingers from my shirt and pushing him towards my dresser until we're standing right in front of it. "The second drawer. It's yours now," I say, and I think my voice shakes a little, but never fucking mind.

"It's mine," he states matter-of-factly, then turns, looking at me. "What do you mean, it's mine, East?"

"Just what I said." I smirk. "It's yours. For your stuff." He tilts his head, then licks his lips.

"But I don't have any stuff. *Here*."

"Of course you do." I gesture at the second drawer. "Now, be a good, obedient Bunny and open it." He shivers, a flush blooming across his cheeks.

"Yes, Master," he says, and my hardness makes it to an entirely new level, ready to burst through the fabric of my pants. I just manage to bite back a needy growl because this is not about me. This is about him. He reaches out and wraps his fingers around the handle, slowly pulling out the drawer. An entire rainbow of colours appears in front of us. First, there's baby blue, then bumblebee—yes, Meredith told me because, to me, yellow is just fucking yellow.

"East?" his voice trembles. "East, what is this?" I can tell that he's seconds away from tearing up; the small, telltale sniffles a sure sign.

"Go on, darling." I nudge him, pressing a gentle kiss against his hair. "You're only halfway there."

"Halfway where?" he asks, bewildered, and I bite back a laugh because, damn, he's just too fucking cute.

"Hmmm," I nibble on his left earlobe. "Get on with it. I have plans with you," I say, digging my hard-on into his crease, eliciting a deep moan from him.

"Yes, Mas—Master," he stammers, his fingers shaking as he pulls the drawer out even more, revealing the next colour. Pear. Then comes bright lilac and, at the very end, an entire palette of pinks. Lace, melon, and peach. Sea, flamingo, and taffy. I memorised all the names, but don't ask me which is which because I have no fucking clue.

"So many," he breathes in awe, tears clinging to his lashes. "Are they all for me?"

"They are," I say, pulling out a pair of the pink ones, little bunnies adorning the soft cotton fabric. He gasps, sending off an avalanche of tears down his cheeks.

"East. They're...I don't...But how?" he blabbers, reaching for the briefs like they're the *Jewels of Lima* or some shit like that, then pulling back as if he's afraid they'll disintegrate at his touch. "There are bunnies," he says, and I laugh.

"There are pandas, too. And baby giraffes." I smile, pushing out my chest with pride. Making him happy is fucking addicting.

"There are?!" he squeals, clasping his hands together in front of him. "I love baby giraffes." He beams.

"I know." I laugh even harder. *I love you.*

"You don't know that," he giggles, finally closing his fingers around the briefs taking them from my hand.

"I do." He shakes his head at me, murmuring something that sounds like '*silly Master,*' before he buries his face in the brand-new briefs, breathing them in.

"There are so many of them," he muses when he eventually comes back up for air.

"There are just enough of them," I say. "Now you never have to worry, my sweet darling. Not about anything."

He nods quietly. I know what's going through his mind right now. He's worried I might mean it right now, but that, with time, it will become something that will make me think less of him. Oh, how wrong he is. Doesn't he know that his vulnerability is one of the things I love the most about him? The fact he needs me, that I get to take care of this precious being I do not deserve, but will keep anyway.

"Nothing," I say. "Nothing will ever make me change my mind about you, Benjamin." He smiles softly, his gaze coasting along the rainbow of briefs.

"It's like we're…" he hesitates, and I can't help but wish that he was wearing his bunny ears. *Later. Later, I'll dress him up, and we'll play.*

"What, darling?"

"It's like we're pee-pared," he says with a snort.

"Jesus," I groan.

"Where did you get them?"

"Oh. Meredith's place. She only just had them delivered last week. Said they'd be high in demand this spring or something like that." He nods, dumbfounded at first, then smiles.

"She does have lovely things...shit, I still owe her for the shirt!" He looks mortified, his eyes spilling over with newfound shame.

"The shirt?"

"The green one," he says. "You know, the one you couldn't stop staring at, East." He blinks innocently. "Like you wanted to tear it right off me and stomp on it." Right. So he *did* notice that. My mortal enemy number one.

"Oh, that one," I grunt. "We can pay for it next time." I shrug.

"Next time?"

"Yeah, I ordered you some more stuff," I say, remembering how I pretty much ordered everything soft, delicate, and pastel-coloured from the spring catalogue that Meredith showed me.

"You did?" he blinks eagerly, dabbing at the tears on his cheeks with the bunny briefs.

"Yeah," I say, playing it cool like I didn't just become 'Customer of the Decade' down at *Meredith's Modern Men's Wear.* "Now, put those back and open the next one."

"The next one?" he looks close to bursting, or tearing the bunny briefs to shreds or perhaps both.

"Yeah. The third drawer is yours, too."

"It is?" he squeals, and I groan, rubbing at my forehead, pushing the second drawer in and pulling the bloody third one out myself because, for fuck's sake, we don't have all day. I have plans for him. His eyes grow impossibly wide as he takes in the content. I placed all his bunny stuff neatly inside it. His ears and wristbands.

His lingerie and stockings. The plug with the fluffy tail. "Master," he murmurs. I reach for the very back and pull out the furriest and, frankly, ghastliest piece of clothing I've ever seen, but again, this is not about me, and I know Benjamin will faint or squeal or most likely both once he realises what it is.

And I'm right. Kind of. When I unfold the adult-sized pale-pink bunny onesie and hold it up between us, an animal-like screech tears from his lips and he starts bouncing up and down.

"Ohmygaaawd, Eeeaaast!" he cries, making grabby hands at the pink horror. "I always wanted one of these!" Of course he did. *Hallelujah, praise Amazon.* I had it delivered last week but hadn't found the right time to give it to him yet. "Can I put it on?" he pants, near-drooling. "Can I, Master?" He blinks. "I know you want to fuck me real bad." He gestures at the clear outline of my fat cock behind my pants. "But I just wanna try it on and then you can tear it right off again."

"No need." I smirk, turning the onesie around and presenting him with the back. His eyes go wide and crimson washes across his cheeks, down his chin, and all the way down his neck. His right hand flies to his crotch, and he looks like he's close to coming, his gaze fixated on the flap on the back, just where the bunny's bottom is.

He leaps into my arms, and I just manage to catch him, before we both stumble towards the bed, landing so that he's straddling me. Showering me with kisses, he pulls at my shirt, the top two buttons flying off, the sound of fabric tearing.

"Thank you, thank you, thank you!" He presses the words against my skin, his breath warm and moist against my collarbone. Then he sits up, his hair deliciously ruffled, his eyes swimming. "Don't go anywhere."

As *if*. "I'll be right back," he pants, before sliding down my body.

"Where're you going?" I grit out. I'm so horny I think I'm going to pass out or suffer an acute implosion of the balls, if that's even a thing. He clutches the bunny onesie against his chest as he backs towards the bathroom, his eyes glued to my massive erection.

"Stay right there," he says, smiling. "Get naked." Then he seems to catch himself. "Please, Master. I'll be right back."

Chapter Nineteen

I could've easily undressed and put the bunny one-sie on in front of East, but the truth is I needed a minute to myself. I rest my hands against the cool porcelain of the sink, my skin flushed and heated. I close my eyes and focus on my breathing. *In and out. In and out.* Like small, soothing waves, my breath calms my body, my heart stilling from the frantic speed with which it was beating. This day. It started with my heart breaking into a thousand little pieces at the thought of having lost him. Lost everything. And now... it's still hard to wrap my mind around it. That he wants me. Truly wants me. I suck in another breath.

There. Better. I exhale deeply, blinking my eyes open, my reflection slowly appearing in the mirror in front of me. What this spectacular man sees in me, I'll never understand. Not in a million years will I understand why he's chosen me, Benjamin. But the fact is, he does see something in me. And not just that. He *sees* me. He truly sees me and the bunny onesie that's waiting for me on the toilet seat is solid proof of that.

When I enter the bedroom, my master is waiting for me on the bed in all his glorious nakedness. Inches and inches of golden skin, his pink nipples standing out like two beacons, beckoning me towards him. He's stroking himself in controlled, languid movements, his right hand loose around his cock, caressing the glistening cockhead on each upward stroke. His left hand cradles his heavy balls, fondling them absentmindedly. God, he's eroticism personified, my Master. I wonder if he knows how powerful his presence is. What it does to me. How it brings out the beast in me who just wants to be claimed and bred and consumed.

He sucks in a breath when he sees me, his icy-blue eyes like liquid fire dancing before me. I'm like a moth to a flame as I float across the room, wrapped in a cloud of pink fleece, a protective cocoon against the outside world. There's only us. He smiles at me, his pink lips separating and his tongue dipping out, licking along his bottom lip as a deep moan escapes him. A generous dollop of precum oozes from his cockhead and he catches it and rubs it up and down his hardness in lazy strokes.

"Darling," he says, his voice strained like he's barely hanging on. My dick hardens, my hole clenching with the need for him to fill me with that fat cock. To split me right open until my hole is moulded around his length, my insides forever changed around him. Just like I'm forever changed by him, my beautiful East. "Look at you," he grits, his eyelids heavy, his cheeks painted a scarlet red. "Look at you, my beautiful, darling Bunny."

"You like?" I shake the hood with attached bunny ears, wiggling my nose. A deep growl and a hissed *fuck* are the only reply I get. East strokes himself faster, his chest heaving, a pool of sweat gathering between his pecs before it starts cascading down his abs like a river of need.

"Turn around," he demands as he scoots backwards, sitting up slightly against the headboard, his right hand still wrapped firmly around his cock. It's an intense red now, a fat purple vein running from the base all the way up to the swollen cockhead. It's pulsing angrily like it's ready to burst and I lick my lips, my mouth watering for a taste, a chance to track that pulsing vein with the tip of my tongue, feeling how it vibrates with his need for me. "Bunny," he groans.

"Yes, Master," I obey softly, like the good bunny I am. As I twirl around, I shake my bunny butt teasingly and another pained *fuck* floats towards me. With my back to him, my instincts take over. I'm prey, waiting for the wolf to hunt me down and devour me. I shiver with need, the inside of my bunny onesie already wet and sticky around the crotch area.

"Shit," he pants. "Shit, shit, shit." The *slap-slap-slap* of his hand against his cock echoes off the bedroom walls. "Perfect," he moans. "You're so goddamn perfect."

My chest swells and does a happy bunny bounce in my chest. *I'm perfect. My Master thinks I'm perfect, and therefore, I am. His word is the law that I abide by. His word is the only thing that matters. His word is my only commandment.*

"Bend over," he coaxes, and I instantly fold at the hips, bending over until my nose meets my legs easily. I'm flexible from hours and hours of garden work, crouching among the rows of vegetables while weeding and caring for the tiny sprouts.

"Show me," he says, an edge to his voice that goes straight to my balls. "Show me what's mine."

I whine in response, my hands flying to my butt, my fingers searching eagerly for the small buttons that are securing the flap. I struggle to unbutton the first one, my fingers shaking, and he must notice, because he hums, "There's a good Bunny. You're doing so well. Your Master is so very, very proud of you."

Oh fuck. I think I have a mini orgasm right then and there. He's proud of me. My Master is proud of me. I sigh with relief as I manage to release the first button, then the other one, the flap opening and revealing my hole for him. I still, holding my breath, my ears trying to make out the nuances of his heavy breathing. I'm so attuned to him. I exist only because of him; I realise that now. My parents never had any real power over me. It was all an illusion. I was always his from the very beginning. And I think I say it out loud because he chuckles deeply.

"Of course you were, my darling Bunny. You were always mine. I just needed to find you and bring you home."

Home. Home, home, home, my body hums and tears spring from my eyes.

"I am home now, am I not, Master?" I sniff, tears cascading into my hair, blood rushing through my head, so loud; like an angry ocean wave crashing against the shore.

"Yes," he sighs, and I hear the trace of vulnerability in his voice. "Yes, my heart. You are home now. You've come home to me." And that's it. I know I'm being naughty. That I'm breaking the rules. But he can punish me later for being a bad bunny. I can't be away from him any longer. It's simply not possible. I stand up and turn around way too quickly, the room spinning all around me, my legs threatening to give way beneath me. Then my gaze connects with his and ever so lightly, barely noticeably, he tips his chin, nodding. I rush towards him, stumbling onto the bed ungracefully, falling against his broad chest. He laughs deeply, happily, as he wraps his arms around me, burying his face against my neck.

"God, you're fluffy," his chest rolls with laughter, his cock digging into my stomach. I nod against his chest as I breathe him in, his musk and sweat doing things to me I can't describe. My hole clenches, begging to be filled by his fat cock, to be owned completely and turned inside out.

"Please, Master. Please," I whimper, brushing my nose against his soft chest hair. "Please fuck me. Please fuck your Bunny," I'm begging him, grinding my cock against his thigh. He laughs again, his hands digging into my hips, attempting to slow my frantic movements.

"I thought I was in control," he muses. "Are you being a bad bunny now, making up new rules?" There's no trace of annoyance or anger in his voice, only fondness and longing.

"I'm sorry, Master. I don't mean to be a bad Bunny," I whine. "I want to be good for you, only good. But..." I lift my face from his chest and blink at him. "I haven't been fucked for so long." He raises a brow at me, a smirk playing along his full mouth.

"Is that so?"

"Yes," I nod eagerly.

"Didn't I fuck you good enough last night?" He frowns.

"You did!" I rush out. "You did. So good. It's just..." Shit, flames lick up my neck with equal parts embarrassment and lust.

"Just what?"

"I'm just so needy for you, Master." I gulp. "All the time," I admit. "It's all I ever think about. How empty I feel."

"Fuck," he growls, digging his cock into my stomach. "Will you behave then?" I bob my head up and down, the bunny ears flopping all over the place. "Is that what you need to behave?" he coos, rubbing his hand behind my bunny ear, petting me gently. "You need to be fucked?" I nod eagerly, one ear plumping into my forehead. "You need your Master to fuck the bad little bunny right out of you? Is that what you need?"

"Yes, please," I squeal. "Please, Master. Please. I'll be good then. I promise. I'll be good."

"You will, won't you? You'll be at my beck and call if I give you my cock, won't you, darling?" His blue eyes gleam, a deep indigo now, a feral promise in them.

"I will," I agree, not just to this, but to everything. "Anything you want, Master. Just please..."

"Anything?" he teases and I nearly come then and there.

"Anything. Always," I promise, sealing our fate.

"Always," he repeats, wrapping his hand around my neck and plunging his tongue into my mouth without warning. I open for him, all air leaving my lungs as he plunders my mouth, sucking my tongue against his. He's wet and warm, and all things dirty and delicious. He gives my throat a test squeeze before his hands slide from my neck, over my shoulders, and down my back. He pauses on the way, teasing me through the fluffy fabric, humming appreciatively. When he reaches my hips, he hesitates, then moves his hands down my thighs, digging his thumbs into my bones. I whine, because fuck my thighs. I want his fingers on my butt, in my hole, fucking me. He laughs again, releasing my mouth, licking down my chin and around my Adam's apple, sucking it into his mouth, slurping greedily around it.

"Arghhhhh," I scream, humping him, my dick hurting so badly now. I want to come and I want his cum in me. That's what I want. Fuck foreplay.

He releases my Adam's apple with a pop and chuckles. "Impatient, are we, Bunny?"

"*Pleeease*," I beg, coming apart on top of him, tears trailing down my face. He pats my thighs, then moves his hands towards my butt. Digging his fingers into the fleshy globes, he wiggles my butt, my hole buzzing with need. His right hand then pulls away and holds up his index and middle fingers in front of my mouth.

"Suck," he demands. "Make them nice and wet." I nod over-excitedly because, yes, fucking *finally*. Sucking his fingers into my mouth, I run my tongue up and down, covering them with saliva. He pushes his fingers all the way to the back of my tongue, teasing my throat, and I gag around them. He hums, fucking my throat, tears streaming down my cheeks. "There's a good Bunny," he smiles. "There's my good little Bunny." I nod, swallowing as drool gathers in my mouth, then eventually spills from my lips and mixes with the tears as they slide down my chin and neck. I'm a mess, but I don't care because I'm *his* mess.

When he's satisfied that I've done a good job, he pulls them out of my mouth and holds them up in front of me. "Ready?" I nod.

"Yes, Master. I'm ready. Please." Then his fingers disappear, and within seconds, I feel their wet coolness at my hole, prodding at the sensitive skin. I jump, but his other hand steadies me, a firm grip on my left butt cheek.

"Easy there." He smiles, leaning in, resting his sweaty forehead against mine, and I instantly relax. "There's a good bunny," he praises me. "Relax, darling." I close my eyes, focusing on my breath and the feel of him against me. His fingers circle my hole, slowly at first, until they start prodding carefully at my entrance.

"East!" I whimper, chasing his fingers, my balls ready to burst and shoot my release all over my onesie. The need to touch myself, to stroke my dick, becomes overwhelming, but I can't. There's no way. I'm trapped. His fingers circle my rim, around and around until I start spinning, too, blood rushing in my head. He licks at my lips, demanding entrance, and the moment I open for him, his fingers breach my hole, the sweet sting soothed by his tongue against mine. He waits until I've adjusted to his fingers, then starts fucking me in slow, deep strokes. Within seconds, I'm riding his hand, leaking like a faucet.

"So eager," he tsks appreciatively against my lips. "So wet for me, my sweet, sweet Bunny." I nod, my eyes squeezed tight as I focus on the stretch. There's no pain now, just a dull throbbing sensation and then the promise of pleasure, all-consuming and infinite. "You're such a little nympho, aren't you?" He bites my bottom lip and I whine. "Such an insatiable little nympho." I nod affirmatively, riding his fingers, my dick catching some friction against the fluffy fabric.

"I am," I sob. "I need you, Master." He curls his fingers inside me, rubbing against my sweet spot and I scream, my lungs echoing the sound. "*Arrgghh!*" He continues to stab at my prostate, pulling animalistic noises from my lips, licking up and down my neck, and occasionally digging his teeth into my skin. Then, just when I think I can't take anymore, his fingers disappear, my hole clenching with desperation. My Master doesn't fail me, though. Within seconds, his fat, slick cockhead pushes against my rim, and he slides into me with one smooth stroke. I think I scream again, but no sound leaves my lips. I can't hear anything. There's only white-hot pain and pleasure flashing before my eyes.

"So big," I whimper, as he fills me up. "So big, so big, so big. Hurts." I struggle around him, and he freezes for a moment before I continue. "So fucking good. It hurts so good." He relaxes, a sigh leaving him before he starts fucking me. He splits me wide open, my hole stretched to the max, bouncing me up and down on his cock, a firm grip on my hips. And I'm exactly where I'm meant to be, connected with him in the most intimate and all-consuming way. His cockhead rubs against my prostate so good, precum shooting from my slit with each touch.

"This goddamn hole," he grits, biting into my neck again. "This sweet, sweet little hole." Sweat beads across his forehead and I dip my tongue out, tasting him, his essence exploding in my mouth. "You were meant to be fucked *just.like.this!*" He digs the words deep inside me with his fat cock.

"I am," I gasp. "I am."

"This fucking hole," he growls again, biting even harder into my neck, then soothing the sting with his tongue. This is a claiming. There's no doubt about it. It's rough, and it's filthy, and it's permanent. It's his wolf coming out, taking from me what he wants, and I go willingly. The bunny in me needs it. I *need* him.

His thrusts are becoming irregular now, frantic, and I know that he's close. My chest expands with pride over what I'm doing to him, my Master. My hole pulses around his cock. It's like he's determined to fuck my insides raw, and I love that idea. I want to throb and ache for days as he uses my body and my hole, taking what he needs from me.

"This hole," he repeats. "I'm gonna breed this fucking hole. I'm gonna fuck a baby bunny into you. You want that, don't you, Bunny? You want me to breed you?" he croaks.

"Yes!" I scream because I want whatever he wants. And I think I scream that, too, because he stills for a moment, then fucks me even harder, deeper, faster.

"You're mine," he promises. "Every part of you belongs to me now." I nod, my tears leaking into his golden hair.

"Yes," I sigh, happiness filling my chest. "Yours." And then I come. I come harder than I ever have before, my hole squeezing his cock so tightly that he gasps and curses. He follows me over the edge seconds later, yelling his release against my neck.

"*Fuuuck!*" He fucks his cum into me, my sensitive insides quivering around him. "So good," he pants. "So, so fucking good." He slides his tongue up my neck, then along my chin, until he finds my mouth and kisses me reverently. "I love you," he murmurs against my lips. "My darling. I love you so much."

"I love you too, Master," I whisper, and although a thousand sensations inhabit my body all at once, I can't name a single one of them. "You are my purpose," I admit, baring myself completely for him. "There's only you." I feel his smile on my lips, his cock still throbbing inside me.

"There's only you too, Benjamin," he says, pulling away slightly, my name spoken with such tenderness that I can't hold back.

"Did you mean it?" I ask. "That you wanted to..." I trail off, suddenly uncertain, digging my teeth into my bottom lip. His blue gaze zeroes in on my mouth, then coasts across the rest of my face, his eyes eventually locking onto mine.

"That I want to fuck a baby bunny into you?" He winces, blushing adorably.

"Yes," I nod. "Or was that just...was that just something you..."

"Is that something you'd want? One day?" he asks, his eyes darkening. And I can't lie. Not when he looks at me like that. Not when his cum is inside me and the imprint of his teeth is burning on my neck.

"Maybe," I admit. "Yes, maybe one day, I'd want that. With you." He nods slowly, and just when I can't take it anymore and want to blurt, '*just kidding!*' jazz hands and all, he shrugs, then echoes my own words back to me. "I want whatever you want. Nothing more, nothing less."

"Yeah?" I sniffle.

"Sure," he laughs. "Why the hell not?" I giggle at that because, wow, who would've thought? "And it'll finally get my mother off my goddamn back if we start popping out babies." He winks. *Babies.* As in plural. An entire litter, perhaps. I giggle again and snort, because being happy feels wonderful, just wonderful. East winces because he's still inside me.

"You know I can't actually have your babies, right?" I grin stupidly, then yawn, feeling a beginning fatigue overtaking my well-fucked, sated body.

"I know," he says, and he actually looks sad for a moment. Then he brightens, regarding me just as stupidly. "Doesn't mean we can't try."

Chapter Twenty

"**I**'m really sorry," he dips his head, glancing at his hands in his lap.

"Will you cut it out?" I chuckle. "I'll get you a new one. Fuck, I'll get you ten." Yes, the bunny onesie is ruined. But fuck, did we have fun ruining it. And although Benjamin looks crestfallen right now, it was as much my fault as it was his. Sure, his cum ruined the fabric in the front, but I was the one who tore off the bunny's butt when he tried to get out of bed and I forcefully pulled him back.

"Really?" He perks up, looking at me, his grey-brown eyes wide.

"Sure." I shrug. *I'll get you anything you want.* At this rate, I'm already headed for an Amazon Gold Member Card.

"Okay, East." He smiles at me in that way of his that makes me want to slam the brakes and pull the car over this very minute and fuck him senseless. I don't care where or when or who sees us. He belongs to me now and I'm a needy bastard. As far as I'm concerned, the rest of the world can either watch me tear my Bunny's hole apart or fuck the fuck off. My fingers tingle to just swerve onto the hard shoulder and put the '*Attention! Emergency Fuck Ahead*' light on. Ugh, I wish, but if there's one thing my mother hates, it's tardiness. She won't have it, and we're already running late because Benjamin had a breakdown of epic proportions when I told him that 1) yes, we definitely ruined the bloody bunny onesie and 2) I forgot we were invited to lunch at my mum's house. Yes, *we*. That was her final demand before she hung up two hours earlier, '*Don't be late, Easter, and remember to bring that darling boy of yours.*'

Mum greets us from the doorstep, waving her arms like a bloody marshaller, as if I've caught a case of amnesia overnight and forgotten where I grew up. Her rainbow-striped apron sparkles in the bright spring sun and I instantly feel bad for not appreciating her more. As far as mums go, I've won the fucking lottery. It's not that I don't. Appreciate her, I mean. I'm just bad at telling her. How much I love her. As she starts jumping up and down, her lips shaped into that '*yoo-hoo*' of hers, I vow to tell her before I leave today. I know she still carries a lot of guilt from back when Dad died, but now that I know what it's like to truly love someone, I can't seem to hold on to any leftover resentment towards her.

"Your mum's a rainbow," Benjamin snorts and starts humming '*She's a Rainbow*' by the Rolling Stones. I smile at him like a loon, forgetting myself and where I am, randomly blurting, "You're the sun." He turns in my direction so quickly that he nearly headbutts me. "Reaally? I'm the sun?" he looks at me wide-eyed, shifting in his seat. Oh, dear God, this Bunny is one B from blowing in his pants already. We need to get this show back on track and commence *Mission: How to Survive Lunch with your mum without fucking your Bunny on the Table.*

"Right," I grunt, wiping my hands roughly across my face. "Let's go, darling."

We quickly disembark from the car and make our way towards my personal cheering squad, aka Mum. Bunny lingers a few steps behind me as we walk across the lawn in front of Mum's bungalow. Spring flowers are starting to burst through the crisp green carpet, and Benjamin *oohs* and *aahs* eagerly telling me their Latin names, most of them something with *vulgaris*. For fuck's sake.

"Darlings!" Mum storms towards us as we reach the house. "Let me take a look at you!" She beams, and I brace myself for her *mum attack*, scrunching my nose because that is a scientifically proven defence against mum kisses. But she breezes right past me, like I'm day-old toast, heading straight for Benjamin. "There you are!" she coos, wrapping him in a rainbow hug and rocking him from side to side. He looks helplessly at me over her shoulder, his eyes wide, dark brown curls all over the place, sparkling as they catch the sun.

"Just go with it," I say, smirking. "Don't fight it. It'll only spur her on." He blinks at me, then relaxes into her arms, his eyelids fluttering closed. My poor darling. It will take some time and a lot of reassurance, but I'm determined to convince him he has a family now. He has me and Mum. And Mr Harvey, of course. He's already texted me twice this morning asking about Benjamin. Maybe we'll bring Mr Harvey with us the next time we visit Mum. That'll keep her somewhat pacified.

Minutes later, we're placed around a lavish table. It's clear that Mum has outdone herself, making sure all my favourite dishes are here, along with a wide range of vegetables. Yes, *someone*, as in *besot-ted-boyfriend-of-the-year*, may have dropped a few hints about Benjamin being a veggie fan. Benjamin takes it all in, his gaze coasting along the beautifully set table and the steaming, delicious dishes.

"You go on now, sweetie," Mum smiles at him. "Don't be shy. If you see something you like, grab it." She winks. Benjamin blushes, his eyes locking on mine, and I just nod and smile because what can you do when you're sitting across from the man of your dreams?

"Thank you, Mrs Bennett," he says softly. "Everything looks wonderful." He swallows audibly and my cock hardens in my pants.

"Call me Dot," she chirps like some 1940s *femme fatale*. What the hell? Dot?

"Dot?" I muse, reaching for the rosemary-roasted lamb chops.

"Sure," she says, shrugging. "Why not? I can be a Dot, right Benjamin? Don't you think I look like a Dot?" She pushes a golden curl off her forehead. Benjamin nods eagerly, sitting up as straight as a ruler. "Yes," he breathes, licking his bottom lip. "You can definitely be a Dot. Like Dorothy Lamour," he says solemnly. "I bet she went by Dot on occasion." What the fuck is happening?

"Dorothy Lamour," Mum exclaims triumphantly, glaring at me. "See? Benjamin knows what he's talking about, don't you, sweetie?" Then she starts singing, "*My heart keeps crying*," and Benjamin chimes in with something that sounds like, "*I'm all a-tremble over you.*" Mum laughs, then lifts her glass, gesturing for us to do the same, clinking her glass against Benjamin's first, then mine. "Here's to Dotty and to l'amour!"

"To love," I grumble, because I refuse to toast to a 1940s starlet named Dotty. Or Dorothy. Or whatever. Mum puts down her glass, her gaze coasting across the table.

"Here." She reaches for a dish of what appears to be honey-glazed zucchini and shoves it in Benjamin's direction. "Have a zucchini. Or two," she giggles. "I can't believe my Easter brought home a fellow lover of classic Hollywood cinema. Who's your favourite?" she continues.

Benjamin blurts "Hedy Lamarr! Or Lauren Bacall. Don't make me choose, Dot." My heart warms at seeing how relaxed he is now, compared to the nervousness pulsing off him in the car.

"*Don't make me choose,*" Mum laughs. "I would never." She holds a hand to her chest, and I think I have a mini-stroke. "You're not eating, darling." She tilts her head at me. "Why aren't you eating, Easter? You look flushed, darling. Are you coming down with something? You should eat."

"I'm eating." I pout like a kid who has just had his favourite toy stolen right in front of him, stuffing a huge piece of rosemary lamb into my mouth and chewing it spitefully.

"Good, good," she muses. "How's the zucchini, Benjamin? You *do* like zucchini, right?" Benjamin hums around a generous mouthful, his eyelashes fluttering in near ecstasy, sticky golden honey dripping down his chin, and I think I whine because Mum looks at me funny. Benjamin's eyes connect with mine across the table, a sudden devilish spark in the light greyish-brown. Licking his lips exaggeratedly, he half-moans, "It's absolutely divine, Dot. You nailed it!"

"Oh, stop." Mum, who's still wearing her rainbow apron, beams brighter than the sun. Then directed at me, Benjamin continues, "I just love a big juicy zucchini." That little incubus! "Wanna taste, East?" He blinks at me, feigning innocence, his grey-brown eyes ablaze. "Or are you more of a turnip kinda guy?" He smiles endearingly, pushing a plate of oven-baked turnips in my direction.

"Look how plump they are," he murmurs. "I bet they'll just melt right on your tongue."

"Oh, they will, darling. They absolutely will," Mum joins in on what has proven to be either 1) the day Easter Bennett came in his pants at his mum's lunch table or 2) the day Easter Bennett choked on a piece of roasted lamb. "You should try them with the gorgonzola sauce." She clasps her hands together with glee. "It's so creamy and salty and I think I really nailed it this time."

"I bet you did, Dot." Benjamin smirks at me, confident and glowing. *I did this*, my heart gallops. My love did this, and it's the most powerful rush ever. It's like a drug to witness the proof of my love for him. How he's changing, transforming right before my eyes into this confident creature. "I bet you *nailed* it," he smiles.

"Have some." She reaches for the sauce.

Oh, he's so gonna get it later and I make sure to mouth it to him across the table. *You're gonna get it.*

"Don't threaten me with a good time, Dot." Benjamin grins at my mother as he accepts the sauce, but I know it's directed at me. "Yummy, yum, yum!" He smacks his lips as I dig my knife into a turnip, stabbing it furiously. I'm gonna wreck that hole later. I'm gonna make it sing around my cock as I fuck my cum into him. Then, when that little pink pucker is drooling with *my* gorgonzola sauce, I'm gonna fuck him again. And again. And again.

"Save some appetite, darling," Mum warns when I stuff a whole turnip into my mouth, the blasted gorgonzola sauce exploding on my tongue. Fuck, it *is* good. "There's *spotted dick* for dessert," she says, putting the final nail in the coffin. Benjamin snorts a mixture of zucchini and gorgonzola sauce, his eyes watering. "There, there." Mum pats him on the back a couple times. Then she looks at me, her eyes watery. "He really is lovely, darling. You did good, Easter. I'm proud of you."

My elaborate and, dare I say, genius plan to finally shut Benjamin up is slowly but surely falling to pieces. I thought he'd be terrified, or at the very least, stunned into silence by the massive dark chocolate dildo that I made just for him. But he simply regards it with awe and hunger, licking his lips hungrily.

"Is that for me?" he moans, and I nearly drop it to the floor. I nod. "Wow, East. It's even bigger than your mum's zucchini." I cringe, trying to wipe that image from my mind. I might need bleach. Or acid.

"Please don't say *zucchini* and *mum* in the same sentence, Benjamin," I groan.

"Ooops." He grins, looking smug, like a cat who caught a canary dipped in cream. "Sooo," he muses, his gaze running up and down the dildo, tracking the fat vein that I carefully moulded into it. "Are you just gonna stand there, waving it around, or are you gonna fuck me with it, Master?" Jesus.

I love this version of him. The one that exudes confidence and a sexy-as-fuck brattiness. My chest bursts with pride and a sense of overwhelming contentment. I did this. I made him believe in himself and the power of his sensuality.

"Just because you wrapped my mum around your little finger, doesn't mean you get to tell me what to do," I warn, raising a brow at him. "Last time I checked, I owned that ass, and if yesterday wasn't a good enough reminder of that, then I guess I'm just going to have to show you again, won't I?" I keep my voice low, as I move towards him. "Now, be a good little Bunny and get on your knees for me."

He nods eagerly, heat flaring in his eyes and last night's love bites glowing on his neck against the paleness of his skin. They'll stay for days and when they fade, I'll mark him again. And then again. An image of Benjamin wearing a pink leather collar flashes before my eyes, and I just know I'll be prowling Amazon later when he's asleep next to me like the possessive motherfucker that I am.

"Yes, Master," he breathes, his eyelids heavy with need. "I'll be a good Bunny now. I'll be *very* good," he promises as he drops to his knees in front of me. He regards me wide-eyed, his head tilted back, as he awaits my next move. I frown because something's off. "What's wrong?" he asks, scooting towards me on his knees, leaning in, resting his left cheek against my right thigh. My hand flies to his hair on instinct and I pet him gently.

"Your ears," I grunt. "Wait right here." Reluctantly, I release myself from him and sprint out the back door and upstairs. Rushing down the hallway, my skin itches to be with him again. It's dreadful, really. It's like a sickness, this urge to be next to him all the time. In my bedroom, I pull out the third drawer, rummaging frantically through the flimsy, fluffy content until I find his bunny ears. My heart settles somewhat and I hurry back downstairs.

My heart nearly melts in my chest when I see him, still kneeling on the floor in the exact spot where I left him. His pants are stretched around his hard-on, his hands clenching and unclenching at his sides.

"Here we are," I hum as I move towards him and carefully place the bunny ears on the top of his head.

"There's my Bunny." He near-purrs, leaning in against me again, seeking the connection.

"Here I am, Master," he says. "*Your* Bunny." I grab the chocolate cock from the counter, moving it towards his mouth. Although we're hidden behind the counter, tucked away from the outside world, I'm still conscious of the fact that the nice, warm spring evening has brought the people of Nettle Green out into the streets. My cock hardens at the thought of fucking Benjamin in the town square in front of everyone, claiming him as mine. Would he let me? If I asked him to? I'm sure he would, but I know I'm way too possessive for that. No fucking way anyone is gonna see what's mine.

Pinning his chin between my thumb and index finger, I tilt his head so his neck is bared for me. Softly at first, I slap the chocolate dildo against his left cheek and he moans loudly, wantonly. He tries to turn his head to taste it, but I tighten my grip around his chin, tsk-tsking at him. "Not yet." He groans impatiently, but complies. "Yes, Master." I slap him again, this time a little harder, and he whines needily, his tongue peeking from his mouth, licking his lips. I alternate my slaps between both cheeks as he writhes and pants, crying beneath me. He's glorious. Absolutely magnificent in his natural submissiveness. No doubt about it, Benjamin was made just for me.

"Please," he whimpers, his forehead scrunched into a tense frown. "Please, Master."

"You want it?" I grit. "You want my cock in your mouth?"

"Yes!" he gasps. "Please."

"Open your mouth," I order him, and he obeys instantly. "Stick out your tongue. Let me see it." He sticks it out like a good little cockslut, and I praise him, unable to hold back. "There we go. Look at that slutty little tongue. Such a good Bunny." He's a sobbing mess by now, unable to speak with his tongue hanging out like this. I lean in, my breath hot against his left ear. "I'm gonna wreck you on both ends, Benjamin. You know that, right?" He nods furiously, his eyes swimming with need. "You were a naughty Bunny earlier, weren't you?" He whines but nods. "Yes, you were," I hum. "You'll need to be punished for that, won't you?" He nods impatiently, the bunny ears bouncing on his head, drool running down his chin.

I tap his tongue lightly and a deep gurgle leaves his mouth. He tries to chase the chocolate cockhead with his tongue, but each time I pull back, then tap him again.

"*Uggghhh*," he groans, more drool cascading down his chin.

"Impatient, are we?" I smirk. "You want to taste it so badly, don't you, darling?" He digs his front teeth into his bottom lip, muffling a pitiful whine. Reaching my left hand to the back of his curly head, I cradle him, then pry his mouth back open, guiding the cock into his mouth and further down his throat. He slurps, then gags around it. My balls draw up at the sight, my cock begging to replace the dildo. "Take me out," I order him as I continue to fuck his mouth with the dildo. His hands fly to my pants, trembling fingers struggling with the zipper until he manages to free me from first my pants, then my briefs. My cock springs free, but he doesn't touch me. He sniffs, shamelessly breathing me in, and within seconds, the scent of my musk reaches my nostrils and then fills the space around us.

Pulling the dildo away, his mouth is swimming with a deep chocolate colour. "Swallow," I grit and he does, humming with contentment, closing his eyes. "Show me," I say, and he sticks out his tongue, showing me how I've painted it a rich brown. "So fucking sexy," I praise him. Releasing my hand from the back of his head, I wrap it around my cock, stroking it a few times, beads of precum pearling at the tip as it continues to trickle from the slit. I'm so fucking horny, and for a second, I'm tempted to just blow my load on his face and fuck him later.

"Please," he whimpers, leaning in against me, smelling me.

"Did I tell you that you could do that?" I say as I continue to stroke myself.

"No, Master. Sorry, Master. I just..." he trails off, opening his grey-brown eyes.

"You just what?" I taunt him.

"I just really want to taste you." He blinks at me innocently, and I'm done for.

"Stick out your tongue, Benjamin," I say, as I guide my cock to his mouth. He opens wide for me, showing me his tongue, and I trace his mouth with the tip of my cock, painting his lips with my juices. He moans happily, chasing me with his tongue and I can't help chuckling. He has no shame and I tell him exactly just that.

"You have no shame, do you, Bunny? You're just such a horny little beast, aren't you?" He nods, humming his agreement before he sucks my cockhead into the wet heat of his mouth. And it's like heaven and hell at the same time. The bliss and the burning sensation in my balls. I thrust my hips carefully, moving my length in and out. He sucks and slurps and drools like the animal that he is. I alternate between shallow thrusts and deeper ones, teasing his throat, indulging in the feel of him gagging around me. It's the craziest power trip. His eyes water, tears trickling down his crimson cheeks.

Pulling out, I take him in, my love. He whimpers with displeasure but I'm quick to push the chocolate cock into his mouth and he latches on to it like a pacifier, happily suckling the tip. The chocolate's starting to melt, but luckily I made it nice and fat enough to last us all night.

Like before, I lose myself in him. The outside world fades away, the voices from the street bleeding into the background. I lose track of time, as I fuck his mouth with the dildo, then my cock, and then the dildo again. My dick is covered in chocolate drool now, Bunny's saliva gliding down my balls, too. He's still on his knees for me, humping the air, his dick a fat outline behind his pants. I'm impressed that he hasn't come yet. He must be exhausted. I mentally put pink knee pads in my Amazon shopping cart.

"Get up," I rasp, pulling my cock from his mouth. He complains briefly, struggling to his feet, until I flip him around and bend him over the counter, his front facing the street outside. I drop the dildo next to him. It's glistening with his saliva and I can't wait to shove it inside him. Tearing down his pants, I take in his fleshy ass, both pale cheeks littered with goosebumps. I lean in over him, blanketing his shivering body with my much larger one.

"You've been such a good Bunny," I whisper against his neck and he moans.

"Thank you, Master."

"How're your knees?" I ask him, rubbing my hands along his ass, digging my fingers into the fleshy globes.

"They—they're fine, Master," he stammers, shifting on his feet. "Do you...do you think anyone can see us?" he asks, and I hear the edge of excitement in his voice.

"I think they can," I lie and he cries out. "You want my cock, baby? Or you want the dildo first? You want the good people of Nettle Green to see how well you take it? How wide your hole can stretch around it before you scream and come on my cock?"

"Yes, God yes," he begs. "I want it. Please, Master."

Leaning back, I reach for the dildo and spit on it once, twice, then a third time. My spit mixes with the remnants of his, the chocolate glistening deliciously.

"Spread yourself for me," I say, and he manoeuvres his hands down to his ass and spreads the cheeks wide for me. His tight pink hole awaits me, covered by that light dusting of dark hair that I've come to love so much, just like I love every little part of him, my Bunny. I prod my finger against the rosy rim and he pushes back to meet me. Gathering some precum from my cock, I circle the pad of my thumb around his hole, rubbing it in, getting him ready for me. Once I'm satisfied I won't hurt him, I guide the dildo to his hole and slip it in on one long glide. He wiggles beneath me, the tips of his fingers digging into his ass cheeks, as he whimpers and mumbles something unintelligible.

"What was that?" I ask him, pulling the dildo out slowly, before I push it in again, this time with a little more force.

"So good," he sighs, his right cheek resting against the smooth surface of the cherry wood counter. "You always fuck me so good, Master," he exhales. Fucking hell. I thrust harder, fucking him faster with the dildo, getting him nice and loose for my cock. I know I won't last long, but neither will he. He's fucking the counter in irregular movements and I know if I tell him he can come, he'll blow within seconds. Benjamin never needs to touch himself when I fuck him. I can get him there, hands-free, with my cock lodged deep in his hole every time. It's magnificent, the way I can play his body like an instrument, pulling the sweetest sounds from his lips and his pink pucker.

I feel him clenching; the dildo vibrating in my hand, and I know it's time. Reaching under the counter, I fumble for the bottle of lube that I put there when Benjamin started working for me and I started sneaking off for emergency wank sessions during the day. I squeeze a generous dollop into my hand and quickly lather my cock in it, the touch along sending sparks shooting up my spine. Pulling the dildo from his hole, I swap it with my cock before he has a chance to complain. I slam home and Bunny screams, sucking me right into his warmth.

"Yes, yes, yes," he chants. "So good," he slurs. I fuck him fast and hard, my cock throbbing with each thrust. He sobs whenever I jam my cockhead against his prostate, pleasure-pain painted across his face. "Please," he whines. "I need to come. Please, Master." His ass is wiggling as he struggles not to.

"You like that, don't you, my little nympho? You like it when I wreck your ass. When I wreck your ripe little turnip?" Shit, I have no control over what's coming out of my mouth at this point, but this Bunny's onboard the train, full steam ahead to Fuckville.

"Yes!" he screams. "Fuck that hole. Wreck it. Fuck that turnip. Cream me with your sauce. Soak me in it!" Holy shit. Slamming into him a few more times, I feel the familiar burn in my chest, my vision starting to blur at the sides. Blood rushes in my head and I feel it, my orgasm, washing over me like an all-consuming wave of bliss. I shoot my juice inside him and he moans happily, then comes within seconds, his entire body shaking with his own release.

"Aaaarrrrhhhh," he calls out, his lofty voice mingling with my deeper one. "Eeeast," he yells, clenching around me, squeezing my cock in a tight, warm glove.

"Bunny," I croak, my eyes stinging, my throat burning. "My Bunny." I love him so much. More than I ever thought possible. And just like always, we're one body, one soul, one heart. When he speaks, his voice is breathy. "I love you so much, East. So so much." And then I do cry, just a little. Because it's overwhelming as fuck when you never thought there was someone out there just for you, and then suddenly, he's right here. *Everywhere.*

"I love you too, darling," I kiss his damp neck. "I adore you," I laugh and he winces. Carefully, I pull out. His hole is pink and beautifully bruised. Then, when he laughs too, my cum—mixed with chocolate—oozes from his hole. Like fucking *MilkyWay* spread; creamy white and rich chocolate. What a sight. It's like him and me, night and day, light and darkness, the fucking sunshine to my grumpy arse.

"Fucking hell," I curse, then dive right in between his peachy ass cheeks. Licking along his crease, I scoop up my cum with the tip of my tongue, then suck more directly from his pucker. He giggles and squirms beneath me, and I hum against his rim. The taste explodes on my tongue, but I don't swallow. Leaning up, I grab him by the shoulders, lifting him, then spinning him around. He regards me through a haze, his eyes love drunk, hair a mess, and the bunny ears askew like the first time he wore them for me. He looks well-fucked and oh so very, very lovely. He looks like mine, my Bunny.

I lean in and claim his mouth in a fierce kiss, hoping that it conveys everything I feel for him. How grateful I am that he came into my life and brought the sunlight with him. That he brought spring. He opens for me, sucking the cum from my mouth, moaning hungrily. We kiss and kiss like there's no tomorrow. Until there's no cum left. Until he's swallowed it all, the evidence of my desire for him now pooling in his stomach.

The world has gone quiet outside, the good people of Nettle Green now resting in their beds, perhaps kissing their loved ones too. Tomorrow, the rush before the holidays starts in earnest, only three days left until Easter. But for tonight, the world has come to a stop, resting as it bears witness to a love unlike any other. A love between a Bunny and his Master. Between a broody chocolate shop owner and his enchanting assistant. But most of all, a love between two men, two lonely souls, who found their peace and purpose in the other.

Epilogue

One Year Later

I used to think that a name was just a name right up until he gave me mine, *Bunny*, and then later his, *Bennett*. Yes, I'm a Bennett now, and have been for a little over two months. Funny how life just seems to sort itself out when you start living it. When you find your place in it. When you find... a home. *Him.* Those two words will forever be irrevocably tied together. *Him* and *home.* I can't think of the one without my mind automatically going to the other.

So, I'm practising until I'm happy that it looks perfect. *Bennett.* I snort to myself because now I am, too, a character in a Jane Austen novel. And not just any character, no, I'm the hero of my own story. The captain of my own ship. And East, my wonderful adoring husband, is the wind in my sails. Yes, it sounds cheesy, I know, but it's my life now. It's a romance novel and each day with him, my dashing husband, my Master, I get to live out my very own happily ever after.

When I'm almost happy with the *Bennett*, I go back to my list. It's never-ending, just like our immortal love. It goes on and on until my head spins right down a rabbit hole and I get all nauseous and antsy and I just crave him. It's overwhelming, frankly, the sensation, but I know I do the same to him. He's told me many times. How he can be in the middle of putting away some papers in his office, or organising some new delivery from Juan, and then it just strikes him, that craving, that itchy feeling. The *raw* need for the other. Like we, too, are irrevocably dependent upon each other. Like the cocoa plant needs the water. Like the sail needs the wind. Like love needs light and trust and tenderness in order to flourish and grow. I used to think love wasn't for people like me, but now I have it in abundance, because we're both determined to let it grow, nurture it, and keep it safe.

I pick up where I left off yesterday. '*Bunny's List of Bestest Things.*' My black pen stands out against the soft lavender paper, a row of spring flowers lining it at the very bottom. My mother-in-law, Dot, gave it to me for my birthday last year. Both the pen and the paper and a lot of other cute stationary with flowers and birds on it. It was the best birthday ever because I got to spend it with my four favourite people in the entire world; Dot, Mr Harvey, my East, and Penelope. Yes, she was invited too and from the look on her face, one would've thought that she'd been invited to a royal wedding. She's become my best friend. I've never had a real friend before. Mr and Mrs Glass usually don't trust anyone to take Penelope out aside from themselves, but they trust me. Because I make Penelope happy. It's easy to make other people happy when you're happy yourself. That's what most people don't get. Happiness is contagious.

Twice a week Penelope and I go to Mr Harvey's garden and work alongside each other for hours and afterwards East takes us both out for ice cream—or hot chocolate if it's too cold for ice cream. If it was up to me and Penelope, it would never be too cold for ice cream, but my husband is funny like that. He also makes me wear a scarf all the way through April so that I don't catch a cold. Luckily, he has learned to distinguish between my sniffles by now, or I'd be confined to my bed most of the time. I was the week after our wedding—confined to my bed, that is—but that was for entirely different reasons. I know he calls me *his funny little thing*, but I swear, most of the time, he's the funny one, my husband.

I muffle a giggle with my other hand. Husband. *Eeekkk.* Okay, the list. After Dot, I put down Mr Woolly. He's my rabbit. A *jersey woolly*, hence the name. East got him for me for our anniversary when he was just a baby. Mr Woolly, of course. Not East. That would be kind of weird and impossible, too. He's the cutest thing ever, my little guy, with his soft grey fur and his black head and black paws. I love him so much. He makes this squeaky noise whenever I come out into the garden, lifting onto his hind legs, eager for me to pick him up. I told him about his predecessor, Bunny, and how I never thought I'd be happy again after I lost him. Mr Woolly looked at me with his huge brown eyes and I swear I saw a murderous glimmer in them, like he wanted to run off and ravage my mother's rose garden.

After Mr Woolly, I put down my pastel briefs and all my pastel-coloured dress shirts. I have just as many as Jay Gatsby now; even Meredith said she'd never seen as many pastels all at once as when the order East had made came in. Then, of course, we watched the movie.

The original, obviously. East fell asleep halfway through, but I forgave him because I'd kept him up late the night before, testing out a new technique of going down on him.

After putting down Mr Harvey's hugs, followed by lavender tulips, I flip to the next page and grin stupidly. It's already filled, only one word written again and again. East. *East, East, East.* Like always, a lump forms in my throat as I start tracing the four letters of his name. I don't know why I still get this emotional. It just comes over me. Maybe because I never saw him coming. I never in a million years expected someone like him for someone like me. Or perhaps it's because he has stayed true to his promise that *nothing*—absolutely nothing—will change his mind about me. About us. About how he feels about me. That I am his.

Because I did have another accident... as in I peed in our bed. It was after my birthday when I'd had too much champagne. This time, when I woke in the damp, clammy bed, I didn't flee like before. I woke East up instead, just like I'd promised I would. He just kissed me, my East, right on the forehead, before he got out of bed and pulled me right with him. He drew me an orange blossom bath and, while I was soaking and crying tears of gratitude, he changed the sheets and then came and joined me. And held me. I don't cry tears of shame anymore. I've decided to put shame in the past where it belongs, with my parents.

Oh, speaking of my love, there he is, lingering in the door to his office. He looks flushed and I know that look all too well. It is, after all, one of my favourites. It's the 'I *got the craving'* look. It's the 'I *can't help myself and I don't give a fuck what you're doing, Bunny, but I need you right now.'* In a second or two he'll grunt because he thinks I haven't noticed him, although he's all I ever see.

"*Hrrmmm.*" See? Called it.

"Oh, hello there." I smirk, putting the cap on my pen as I look up. "I didn't see you there," I blink in my best Oblivious Bunny fashion. He scowls, mumbling his usual, "don't play with me, Bunny," that goes straight to my balls. Shifting on his office chair, I tap the tips of my fingers against the wooden desk, waiting him out, like I'm some school principal, and he's late for class.

"What are you doing?" he scans the desk, a pretend aloofness to his voice, like he just came in looking for an order or some random piece of paper. *Oh, I see you, Mr Bennett. I see right through you.*

"Making a list," I smile at him.

"Another one?" he sighs, rubbing at the golden scruff on his chin, making my mouth water, my inner thighs burning with the phantom feel of his face buried between them.

"So what if it is?" I swallow down a mouthful of drool. "When you used to have nothing to make lists about, it's nobody's business if you feel like making them all the time." He snorts at that, as he moves inside the office, and up to the desk, where he leans his right hip against it, crossing his muscular arms in front of his chest. Another tidal wave of drool flushes my mouth and I fail to bite back something that sounds like a *mweep.*

"Nobody's business, huh?" he stares at me, raising a blond brow at me, his silent warning making my hole clench like a clam.

"Sorry, Master," I swallow, and heat flickers in his blue eyes. Uncrossing his arms, he moves around the desk until he's hovering right next to me, reaching out his left hand, burying the right in his pants pocket. His fingers dive into my hair, carding through my wild locks slowly. Goosebumps spread down my neck as he pets me, humming contentedly, like he's had his fix. His Bunny fix. Then he leans down and presses a tender kiss to first my forehead, then the tip of my nose, until he finds my lips in a searing kiss that promises the entire world and then some. I feel his smile against my Cupid's bow, his scruff tickling my skin, his familiar scent engulfing me. He hums again, sucking my bottom lip into his mouth, laving at it with his tongue. Then, just like that, he releases my lips, and I find myself panting like a bunny in heat, my butthole twitching.

"Go back to your list, darling," he purrs. "Don't let me keep you." Sorry what? Is he being serious? I wouldn't be able to hold a pen to a paper even if someone slapped me with a carrot. I'm putty. Or not even that. I'm barely *put*.

"The list?" I blurt, dumbfounded. "But...but I thought..." I stammer. "Didn't you want something?" I squeak.

"Oh, it can wait," he says casually, shrugging, looking at his cuticles like they're the most interesting thing ever. And I suddenly hate those cuticles, because what the hell? *Look at me.* Look. At. Me.

"I'm done!" I blurt instead, the pen flying from my fingers, crash landing against the filing cabinet behind me. I'm so done. Done *for*, that is.

"Well, if you're sure..." he trails off, smiling knowingly.

"I'm sure, East," I pant, smiling back at him. "I've never been more sure about anything." And it's true. I haven't. Because the broad smile I'm rewarded with is just everything. *He* is everything, my East, my husband, my Master.

Bunny's List of Bestest Things

1. Dot
2. Mr Woolly
3. Pastel Briefs
4. Pastel-coloured dress shirts
5. Mr Harvey's Hugs
6. Lavender tulips

East East
East East
East East
East
East East
East
East East
East

Epilogue

Some time later...

Although I wouldn't trade my life for anything, I swear I'm too old for this. Bouncing up and down on my toes, I take in the counter that's a right mess; baby wipes, spilled formula, a pair of tiny bunny ears, and toys all over the place. Huxley looks like he's finally hopped off to dreamland, but Lilac still glares at me with her huge blue eyes, her button nose scrunched up like she's smelling something foul. She better not have pooped again—I just changed her diaper for the third time today. Who knew babies were proper poop machines? *Not me,* said the sleep-deprived daddy.

"Aren't you sleepy yet?" I yawn at her and her face twists into that indecipherable baby smile that could either mean a) I'm working on a new diaper for you, fucker, 2) I'm getting ready to scream my head off, old man or 3) You're the centre of my universe, Daddy. I hold my breath, and then, just like that, she yawns, smacks her lips and passes out next to her brother. Oh, thank God. Thank the good old fucking Lord.

Experience tells me that the sheer luck of both of them being out at the same time is the equivalent of *A Hundred Year Flood* or *Halley's Comet*. Within seconds, I move like a ninja, scooping up half-finished bottles and used tissues. Hurrying out back, I dump the pile of shit into the diaper bag, making sure there are still two fresh bottles left in the side pocket, one with a pink cap for Lilac and a sky-blue for Huxley. I accidentally got the bottles mixed up once at 4-something-am and let's just say that Her Royal Majesty, aka my daughter, was not a happy camper. She nearly blew out my eardrums and woke up her other daddy, aka my heavy-sleeper husband.

I rush to the bathroom because taking a leak post-babies is also *A Hundred Year Flood*—pun intended—and my bladder is currently working overtime on not bursting. Perhaps I should just wear a bloody diaper too. Relieving myself as quietly as I can, still bouncing a little, humming *Old MacDonald Had a Farm*, I do a quick mental inventory, making sure I have everything packed and ready for later. Fuuuck, I can't wait to just get the fuck out of Babyville for 48 hours with the most amazing human in history, aka my husband, my Bunny.

Once my bladder sighs with contentment, I pull up my pants and move to the sink. And that's when I glimpse myself in the mirror. Thank God the light in here is dimmed because, holy crap. My blond hair, now with a few sprinkles of grey in it, stands out from my head like I've been electrocuted. There are dark circles under my eyes that would make Frankenstein's Monster green with envy, and my scruff has turned into an almost-beard. A large stain of dried baby drool adorns my right shoulder like a badge of honour, and I only just now realise that I'm wearing my T-shirt inside out. And yet, I'm smiling like a loon, my tired blue eyes glazing over with a layer of unshed tears as I take in Lilac and Huxley sleeping peacefully, snuggled up against my chest in the *Babybjörn Baby Carrier* strapped around my shoulders. Huxley whimpers in his sleep, his long ears twitching, and my heart melts and I turn into goo. I'm so fucking tired, I could sleep standing up for days without end, and still, I'm the happiest I've ever been.

Lilac smacks her lips until they curl into a cute pout. She's only four months old. She's tiny, with dark downy hair peeking from behind the knitted yellow hat that Mum made for her. She's a right monster when she's awake but a pure angel when she finally sleeps. We'd been on the adoption list for eighteen months when they called and told us they had a baby girl for us. She'd been given up for adoption shortly after her teen parents found out that they were pregnant with her.

'Lilac,' Benjamin breathed with awe next to me when I held our daughter in my arms for the first time. '*I want to call her Lilac. Can we? Please East? After Bunny*,' his voice broke, her tiny hand wrapped around his index finger. '*Bunny was a Lilac.*' I just nodded, no idea what he was on about, but going along with whatever he wanted like I usually do because he's my heart. He and Lilac. Huxley too, in some weird way. Later, much later, when Lilac was sleeping on my chest and we were both wiped out but disgustingly besotted with our daughter, he told me about Bunny. How Bunny was a Lilac, which is a very rare but treasured bunny breed. I didn't think it was possible, but at that moment, I swear I felt my heart expanding in my chest, my love for him growing even bigger than before.

'*It's beautiful,*' I whispered into his sweet-smelling hair. '*You are beautiful, my treasured little family.*'

Huxley came a month later, completely unexpectedly, when Mr Harvey found him caught in the butterfly net covering his cabbage. He was fucking tiny, and after Mr Harvey had waited for the baby's mum to show up all day, he eventually brought him home with him. Benjamin took one look at the light brown leveret, and that was all it took for it to become known as '*the day that Bunny convinced his Master they needed a baby hare in addition to a baby girl.*' Needless to say, he managed to convince me. The stuff my husband can do with that tongue of his... *right.* Hopefully, I'll have a chance to get reacquainted with his tongue a few times this weekend. *His hole too, mate,* my cock chimes in. *We're close to busting a nut, arsehole.* Right, right.

Because that's the only downside actually of being one big happy family—your non-existent sex life. I know it'll get better once we're safely out of Babyville, but still, I miss fucking my Bunny in his onesie without having to worry about Lilac screaming her lungs out or Mr Harvey yelling *dinner!*

We all moved into Mr Harvey's house when we found out that we were expecting Baby Lilac. It kind of made sense. Mr Harvey isn't getting any younger and my flat upstairs was only ever meant for one, really. Not an entire family. *An entire family.* Who would've thought a grump like me would end up being a whipped family man, missing my husband the minute he walked out the door?

Speaking of which, he should've been here by now. He was just going to give Mr Harvey—whose given name is actually Frank—a hand building a fenced play area for Huxley in the back garden next to Mr Woolley. I look at my watch. It's only 3:27. Our dinner reservation isn't until eight, but we agreed to give Frank a hand with dinner before we left for the weekend getaway I've booked at a B&B just outside Canterbury. Mum's staying with Frank while we're away. They get on like a house on fire and he always laughs over her questionable vegetable euphemisms, his eyes lighting up whenever she stops by, which is pretty often, come to think of it.

The familiar door bell chimes and I curse. Shit, I forgot to put the 'We're Closed!' sign up. I swear to anything that might exist if some chocolate-deprived customer wakes up the babies, I'll commit murder in broad daylight. Rushing out into the front, my anger evaporates the minute I see him, my Benjamin. My beautiful husband, my baby daddy.

"Hello there, gorgeous." He winks, beaming at me, his cheeks flushed a pretty pink from the spring sun. "I see you're still rocking that *Babybjörn* like a badass daddy," he smirks.

"Hey, you know me," I blow at my index fingers real John-Wayne style, then pretend to be putting my badass airguns back in an invisible holster around my hips. "Chocolatier extraordinaire by day and sexy baby daddy by night."

"It's not night yet," he snorts, then blushes even harder, his eyes darkening with longing.

"Not yet," I muse, moving towards him, catching his lips in a sloppy kiss when I get there.

"Mmmm, carrot," Benjamin hums against my lips, smiling. "How's Huxley getting on with the carrot mash?" He peeks into the baby carrier, a concerned frown between his dark brows, before pressing a tender kiss against Lilac's forehead.

"Better than the porridge," I say and we both wince at the same time and I think I gag a little too. Yeah, that was a regular shit show, pun intended.

"Thank God," he laughs and my heart bursts with happiness. "We can try zucchini next," he giggles, digging his teeth into his bottom lip.

"Jesus, darling. Not here," I croak in a whisper.

"There's no one here," he laughs again.

"The babies," I hiss, my gaze dipping to the sleeping devil's spawn, my hands cupping Huxley's huge ears, sheltering them from my husband's dirty mouth. Benjamin's gaze softens, the greyish-brown now a deep moonstone.

"Awww," he coos. "Look at you." He smiles. "Being all protective."

"Look at yourself," I counter like I'm five or just a grumpy arsehole. "Being all..." I can't think of anything because he is everything.

"No, look at youuu," he teases, sweeping his fingers through my wayward locks. "You look yummy," he moans. "Being a dad suits you."

"You look fucking delicious yourself," I growl, smacking his perky turnip butt and he giggles, his voice a soft trickle, filling the room. And that's how we go, him and I, like the crazy, lovestruck fools we are. We go on and on and on until we forget ourselves and the world all around us. Until there's nothing else but him, my live-in co-chocolatier, my darling husband, the father to my babies, my sweet, sweet Bunny. My heart, my love, my life.

The End

Afterthoughts & Acknowledgments

O ur dearest, loveliest readers,

That's it!

It was Easter and Bunny's immortal love story and we hope that it was everything you hoped it would be. And perhaps even a little bit more. We sure had fun writing it, diving into how you can use your trauma and turn it into something positive and perhaps even playful. How overcoming your trauma can be empowering if you find that special someone who sees you and meets you in it. Like Easter when he sees and embraces Benjamin for who he truly is. That's all we can ever really hope for in life; to be seen and loved for who we are. And Easter gains the world in return; a love so strong and all-consuming that he even forgets that he was supposed to be the grumpiest grump that ever grumped in Kent. And a family, too. Babies! Human babies, animal babies! Isn't life just magical? How it just works out exactly like it was always supposed to be if you follow your instinct and just open your heart. Benjamin follows his instincts and Easter responds by opening his heart. Fuck, we're tearing up just writing this.

Love is beautiful and the essence of everything that connects us with other people. Like you, our dear, lovely readers. We write and you read and then something happens. It sets off a chain reaction. We've gained so many friends through our books. We love all your messages; how our books have made you feel. How you perhaps felt seen or gained a new book boyfriend. We love them all, so keep them coming. Reviews are great, because they bring us new readers but your lovely, funny and sometimes personal messages are what makes us believe that there's a place for our books. It's what we read again on a rainy day when we doubt ourselves and feel like throwing in the towel. You guys matter more to us than you may think.

As two childhood trauma survivors living with our trauma and diagnoses on a daily basis, you've become part of the light that we look for when the darkness tries to consume us. So thank you for that.

Here are other people that bring the light in no particular order:

Our families and friends, of course. Thank you for supporting us on this crazy adventure.

Thank you to our kick-ass amazing friend and PA, aka the Lovely Norwegian, Mariansen PA. Thank you for keeping us on the straight and narrow when we fall into a rabbit hole (pun intended!) or for encouraging us when we go on one of our "We suck so bad and no one wants to read our books" tirades.

To Jenn Green, who has become our lifeline and a wonderful friend; thank you for editing our words and formatting our books. You make them so fluffing gorgeous that we just wanna cry (we do actually cry!). Please never ditch us!

Also a huge shoutout to Regi aka Regitse Liljadorff who not only beta reads for us but also turns our books into stunning art. The way you see our men is just unique and your art is out-of-this world gorge.

A huge thank you to our Street Teams who do a wonderful job posting about our books and upcoming releases. We are so dedicated and amazing that there are no words. If it weren't for you guys sharing our stuff, we'd be thoroughly fluffed.

Thank you to our ARC readers and all our readers in general. It is you guys who sell our books with all your kind reviews or book recommendations.

Also, thank you to this community in general. To all the Bookstagrammers, group admins, and authors who support us in one way or another. We love this queer corner of the world—it is our outlet, our safe space, and a place we treasure so much. It is, after all, where we all met!

That's it... probably. Until next time, which for The Kinkster Sisters, will be in 2026. This time the book will take place in Denmark because Anja is Danish and Danish men have some of the longest schlongs in Europe and a certain British guy just needs to see that for himself. Or feel it. Or taste it. Or ride it. Or whatever. You know us, the sky's the limit.

Love is love,
Anja & Emma

Printed in Dunstable, United Kingdom